BRIGHTON DARKNESS

Other published works by John Roman Baker

Novels
No Fixed Ground
The Dark Antagonist
The Paris Syndrome
The Sea and the City
The Vicious Age

Plays
The Crying Celibate Tears Trilogy
The Prostitution Plays

Poetry
Cast Down
The Deserted Shore
Gethsemane
Poèmes à Tristan

BRIGHTON DARKNESS

John Roman Baker

WILKINSON HOUSE

Brighton Darkness
Copyright © John Roman Baker 2015
The moral right of the author has been asserted.

Published by Wilkinson House Ltd, June 2015

FIRST EDITION
978-1-899713-41-7

Wilkinson House Ltd.,
20-22 Wenlock Road,
London, N1 7GU
United Kingdom

www.wilkinsonhouse.com
info@wilkinsonhouse.com

Cover design: Bobbie Lloyd

Bobbie Designs
cargocollective.com/bobbielloyd

Cover photo by Rod Evan
Astoria Cinema, Brighton, April 2015

British Library Cataloguing-in-Publication Data
A catalogue record for this book is available
from the British Library.

Dedicated to Francis Scarfe,
a fine poet who both helped and inspired other poets.

Je suis comme je suis
Je suis faite comme ça

(I am what I am
I am made like that)

- Jacques Prévert -

Show so
so the wounds on water
The wasted man

- John Roman Baker -

CONTENTS

THE ATTIC

It is a long time ago. I can no longer remember the weather in the streets, or exactly what fashions we wore. I cannot remember the smell of the city or the taste of the food back then. I know it felt and sounded different than it does now. I know young men and women wore clothes that would now make the young laugh, however much they may imitate with retro styles. The dirt, I think, was somehow dirtier, or more to the point, the grime on things. We were not so clean, and yet the nearness of people was more acute, more pressing, and despite the rawness of post-war life there was a freshness in the air. We were modern, or so we thought. But what I can still remember (beyond all the superficial aspects of the passing of time) was the pain I experienced then: the pain that has never gone away, but only draws itself closer to me, to the inner bone of how I think and feel.

It was during the summer months of 1960. Antonioni's *L'Avventura* was playing in the cinema (or had it just been, or was it still to come?) marking a new turning of time, a new decade of seeing. The strict old ways were falling apart, and the fear of the bright unknown was exciting and very, very alive. We all seemed over-sensitive to each other, as if a layer of skin had been stripped away. Even those who clung to older things, to classical studies, Oxford and Cambridge, and Forster to read, were aware of a bright newness, a springtime of being. Nothing seemed absolute anymore; all was in the nature of relativity.

The two who are the subjects of this narrative met in a men's clothes shop close to Kensington High Street. The older of the two was around thirty-two or three, and the younger, a boy of seventeen who had only recently started his job as sales assistant. The older whose name was Derek Hadlam was buying a tie, and the younger whose name was Mark Dean was helping him choose.

"Which one would you choose?" Derek asked, holding up several.

"I think the thinnest one, in black."

"Why?"

"The simplicity of line."

"But don't you think it is too stark? Too black? There's another one here with a touch of grey. It is similar in that it is thin, but the grey touch softens it a little."

Mark looked at Derek and said simply, "You are dressed in a white suit, you have a slim body, and your hair is quite curly and black. Personally, I think the black tie is just right."

He smiled his very young smile and Derek acknowledged to himself how much he was attracted to the youth. He was attracted to Mark's wide open face and to the fact that he was his opposite: rather short, a little stocky, and with blond hair.

"I will take the tie on one condition," he said, "that you choose a tie for yourself."

Mark laughed at this, but not unkindly.

"I have a tie," he said, "and I am forced to wear it. They wouldn't continue to employ me if I didn't wear it. Outside of work I don't wear ties. In fact before I came here I never wore a tie in my life."

Derek was upset by the laughter. He liked manners in people, and this laugh at his proposal of a present felt almost insulting. He wanted to be polite to the youth, to say thank you and leave the shop, but instead he stayed and staring at Mark blurted out the words, "Would you have dinner with me after you have finished work?"

Mark smiled and nodded his head, then said slowly, "Maybe I'm not the right sort of person to choose a tie for you."

Derek picked up the black tie awkwardly.

"It's a fine choice," he replied. "I have a confession to

make though. I have never worn this ridiculous white suit before. It was a present from my mother and I couldn't say no to it. I had lunch with her just before I came here. She made me wear it because, as she put it, it's a lovely summer's day and white is good for summer."

Bending down he picked up a bag and opening it showed a grey sweater and trousers folded neatly inside.

"I normally wear light sweaters in summer and grey or black trousers. It's only for special occasions that I wear a suit—you know, the opera, a dinner with her, or a special day like Henley Regatta."

Mark smiled and said he would meet Derek outside the shop at six. He then carefully wrapped the tie, took Derek's money, and watched as Derek looked at several things in the shop before leaving.

Dinner was at a simple restaurant in South Kensington. Derek had changed into casual clothes. Mark felt awkward as his clothes were more cheaply made. He also felt self-conscious that he was wearing jeans. During dinner Derek told him he was interested in archaeology, and that he was thinking of going on an archaeological dig in the middle-east in October.

"My first," he said. "Some ruins that date back to a Roman occupation."

"I don't really know much about all that," Mark replied, "but it sounds interesting."

"What are your interests?" Derek asked.

"Poetry," Mark said. "I would like to be a poet."

Derek looked at him with pleased surprise. He looked relieved, as if he had met an equal. He was tired of meeting uneducated youths who were only concerned with rock 'n' roll and the worst of American cinema. Their legs brushed under the table and Derek did not move his leg away. He pressed and felt the warmth from Mark's body.

"I suggest we talk more about your interest in poetry back

at my place. I live in Cheyne Walk in Chelsea."

Mark said that he lived over the river in Battersea. Then he made a feeble joke about the dogs home before saying yes, he would like to come back to Derek's place.

Once there he felt more at ease. Derek had a lot of books, including a wide collection of poets. Without asking, he picked out a book of David Gascoyne's work.

"Very forties," Derek observed.

"I like that," Mark said. "I know it's not fashionable at the moment, but I think we might get back to liking the richness of language they had in the forties."

"Do you think we have lost it then?"

Mark nodded his head and replaced the book.

"And is your language rich?" Derek asked.

Mark was not sure if there was not just a trace of mockery in his voice.

"I like to think so," Mark said. "I have sort of visions. Sometimes I even dream whole poems, and when I wake up, some of them are still there." He paused. "That's when I don't get nightmares. But even then, those can end up as material for my poetry."

Derek did not really like going into the darkness of inspiration, so he smiled, poured Mark some coffee and tried to change the subject.

"I don't read as much imaginative work as I perhaps should," he said. "I'm more of a nineteenth century man. Jane Austen mostly and Anthony Trollope. The twentieth century poetry on my shelves was mainly given to me."

Mark felt as if he had been put down and there was a long silence. He looked around the room. It was beautifully furnished, and he especially liked the William Morris wallpaper. Inside he felt a little ashamed of the untidy room he rented, in what Derek would no doubt consider an unfashionable part of London.

"Arts and Crafts," he murmured, showing off his

knowledge.

"Yes, the revival of traditional British textile arts. I'm afraid, once again my mother's choice." Then he paused and added, "How come you have such a good education, yet work where you work?"

Mark put down his cup of coffee. His hand was beginning to shake, and he felt suddenly dizzy. He knew the beginnings of panic attacks well and he was afraid he was about to have one.

"Can I use your bathroom?" he asked.

"Of course. I'll show you."

Derek showed him and discreetly shut the door behind him.

After a while, Mark came out feeling and probably looking much better. Derek went over to him and took him in his arms. They kissed for a long while before Derek led him to the bedroom.

In bed Mark was rather coltish and in some strange way inexperienced. He was shy about oral sex and would not allow Derek to penetrate him. They ended up mutually masturbating, which was less than satisfactory for Derek.

"I'm bad in bed. I know."

Dressed again, in the living room, Mark sat on the edge of a chair facing Derek. He felt too uneasy to sit beside Derek on the sofa.

"It will get better," Derek said simply. "I imagine it was all kind of new to you."

Mark looked at Derek and shook his head.

"No," he answered frankly. "This may sound paradoxical, but I have had quite a bit of experience. But despite that, I feel I have had very little experience. When it comes to sex I am always, it seems, a dead loss. My nerves I guess get in the way."

He looked around the room, trying to avoid Derek's questioning looks.

"Is there something you haven't told me?" Derek asked.

"I had a breakdown," Mark said suddenly. "It was just after my mother died. My father had been separated from her for years, and she was all I had. I seldom see my father. It was when they broke up that my studies went to pieces and I had to leave school."

It all came out in a rush—too much of a rush. Mark gasped and asked if he could have some water. Derek went to get him some and stood rather too patiently over Mark as he drank it down. He hoped Mark was not about to have another breakdown, and he felt frustrated at the way the encounter between them was turning out.

"Did you go to hospital?" he asked.

"No. I was staying at the YMCA in Brighton. Brighton was where my mother and I used to live. I had my first job there. In menswear." He paused, then said slowly, "I sat in my room one evening and quite deliberately and quite coldly took an overdose of Aspirin. I'm not sure how much I took."

Mark's hand began to shake and Derek took the glass away from him hurriedly.

"This is really none of my business," Derek said.

"But you asked."

Mark looked at him and Derek quite unexpectedly felt attracted to the need in his voice. He also realised that contrary to what he wanted to feel, he was very much attracted to him. He liked the soft curve of Mark's face and the colour of his hair. He remembered how, at the moment of sexual climax, he had buried his face in the boy's hair to muffle his cries.

"Yes, I asked," he said. "I am interested in you. Tell me what happened."

"I took the pills and then went to bed and fell asleep. The dreams were terrible and the next thing I knew, I woke up screaming. I was giddy and felt I was going to die. I didn't want to die, despite what I had done."

Mark began to sob then, but waved Derek away as he approached to calm him.

"I got out of bed, crawled down the stairs and out into the empty street. I lay there on the road screaming. Then I remember a few people helping me up and everything was spinning. I told them where I lived and the next thing I knew it was morning and I was back in bed. It was as if nothing had happened."

"But didn't they call an ambulance?" Derek asked.

"I don't know. No. No, of course they didn't. I was put back into my bed by strangers and they left me."

"That's criminal. You should have been taken to hospital."

Mark wiped the tears from his eyes, then added quietly, "Whoever they were who got me back into the house and back into my room, did not want to get involved. I woke up alone, had a long shower and thought I felt better."

"And did you?"

"Yes, until I went out. Once outside I had the strangest sensation. I felt I was two people. I was me, but there was another me walking in front. It was a sort of projection and I had to hurry to keep up with myself. I should have been terrified, but I wasn't. I told myself I would join up with myself eventually and that I was only temporarily divided."

Mark paused. For a while it was too difficult to continue.

"And have you become one with yourself now?" Derek asked.

"Sometimes I feel I have. Sometimes I don't. It's then that the panic starts. I feel I will never, ever again be whole."

"You saw a doctor of course."

Derek knelt down in front of Mark and took him in his arms. Mark simply said to him that he had been too afraid and too alone to see anyone, and that he was afraid of doctors.

"And your father? Does he know?"

"No," Mark said. "No one knows except you."

A few weeks later, Derek and Mark were living together in the Cheyne Walk house. They had fallen in love with each other, or so they said. Derek took Mark out on an almost daily basis. On one occasion he had even taken him to his sister's house. She knew her brother was homosexual and she had liked Mark even if she had shown concern that he was so young.

"It is against the law, you know," she had said.

Derek was aware of that, and afraid of it, but still his love, or perhaps his obsession grew. Even the sex got better. Mark had reluctantly agreed to anal sex as long as he was the active partner, and Derek, who was versatile, enjoyed this: the only passive act on his side of their relationship. Other than that, he more or less controlled Mark. He took him out of the shop where he had been working and by pulling a few strings managed to get him a better paid job in a higher class boutique that was the talk of London. He made sure Mark was dressed well and that he was presentable enough to be taken anywhere.

"Now we must celebrate our living together," he had said.

With a few other gay friends, they celebrated his coming to live in the house with a party. Not all of the guests approved of Derek's choice. His best friend, a theatre critic, told Derek that Mark was intrinsically unstable. Derek asked him how he knew, but his theatre critic friend shrugged his shoulders and said he had seen a lot of instability in the young and that was why he preferred older men.

All was well for a while until the time came for Derek to make plans to go to the Middle East.

"Can't I come as well?" Mark asked.

"It would bore you. And anyway, I'd like you to look after the house."

"I can't be alone at nights," Mark said. "I can't."

"You were alone before I met you, weren't you?"

Mark was silent and Derek realised he had not been told everything.

"So as not to be alone," Mark replied, "I picked up men to sleep with me. I went to the clubs and the parks. If I had to I went with anyone."

Shocked, Derek asked him if he had not been afraid of the police or of disease.

"I rarely took sexual risks," Mark said. "I just couldn't be alone."

With this revelation, Derek began to feel differently about Mark. He didn't want to have sex with him as often, and he no longer told him he loved him. The silence in the house became like a wall between them. Everything Mark did was wrong, and one night he had a panic attack. He felt his body was separating into two again and that he was going mad. He screamed so much that the next day the neighbours began to ask questions.

"This can't go on," Derek said. "You'll have to see a doctor."

As it happened, Derek had a doctor friend who lived in Fulham, and it was arranged for him to see Mark. The doctor's opinion was that Mark was very ill mentally and that he should be admitted for a while to the mental ward of a hospital just outside London.

"Please don't make me go," Mark pleaded, but Derek insisted and smiled, adding that all would get back to normal for both of them once he was cured.

Mark was admitted to the hospital. He was on an open ward with several other men of varying ages. He was given drugs and was so depressed he did not even bother to ask what they were.

"I like you."

A young man on the ward called Peter told him this one day. Peter was in hospital because he could not go out of doors. He was terrified at the prospect of the outside world and could only look at it through windows or doors. He was also good looking and Mark was attracted to him.

"But if I were to take you out into the hospital grounds, would you at least try?"

Tears welled up in Peter's eyes.

"I can't," he said. "I'm ill like the rest and it won't change. Once you're in here you're in for life."

"Nonsense," Mark replied. "Just take a few steps with me in the garden."

Peter shook his head.

"In here," he said, "I would do anything for you, but I can't do that. One step out there and I would collapse."

"Won't you try?"

He realised he was being insistent, but Peter was only a year older than himself and he felt a sense of horror at the life he was condemning himself to. But then, he told himself, the boy is ill. Like me. I am ill. Can I alter just because someone else wants me to?

He spent most of his time with Peter. He even recited some of his poems to him from memory. Peter loved poetry, and this drew them together even more closely. One night before going to bed they kissed each other on the lips.

"I don't know if I am like that," Peter murmured. "I don't know if I am one of them."

"I know I am," Mark said.

"Does it matter? Does it matter if I am?" Peter asked.

"I'm not going to get you into anything," Mark replied.

He kept to his word. He watched over the brown-headed boy as if he was his lover, and there was a certain peace in this unexpected relationship.

Then suddenly in the middle of the night in early October, all the male patients were told to get out of bed for an emergency meeting. A young man on the ward had said he had been raped by a fellow patient, and because of that there had to be an immediate investigation. It was three in the morning and Mark noticed Peter did not want to sit beside him. Endless questions were asked, and the young man said he did not know who it was. He had gone to the toilet. It had been dark in there, and when he had tried to turn on the light a restraining hand had stopped him. He said that then he had been thrown to the floor and his pyjama bottoms had been pulled down.

"My penis was grabbed," the young man cried. "It was made hard forcibly, and a voice told me that if I did not cooperate I would be killed."

"Did you recognise the voice?"

Question after question to which there were no answers. No one on the ward admitted to knowing anything about it.

"Who went to the toilet tonight?"

No one admitted that they had.

It was light when Mark went back to his bed. Peter avoided looking at him. During the day when he approached Peter, he was ignored.

"You don't believe I did that?" Mark asked.

Peter shook his head in silence.

"Then talk to me."

Instead, Peter turned his head away from him and from then onwards would not have anything to do with him.

This lasted for a week. Mark had never felt more alone. He cried every night in his bed and when one morning he was told they were thinking of giving him LSD treatment he decided to run away.

It was easy to leave the hospital, easier than he had expected. He just slipped out of the door one night and walked to the nearest train station that would take him back to London. He boarded a train without any money and upon arrival at Victoria Station walked to Derek's house. Once there he found the house was empty. Of course, he said to himself, he is away. It's October. He's in the Middle East.

He slept rough for a few nights in a park before being picked up by a much older man. The man, whose name was Harold, lived in Kentish Town and took him back to his place. He had about five cats. The place stank of cat piss and the flat was damp and cold. For two nights he held out against having sex with the man, but eventually gave in. It was with this man, out of whatever feeling of desperation or duty that he did not know or understand, that he allowed himself to be penetrated. It was painful and he bled a lot afterwards.

"I can't do that again," he told Harold. "If you force me to, I will leave."

Harold was pathetically grateful for his company and they lived together for a few months. Mark had lost his job when he went into hospital and as the man was out of work as well, they spent their days together. Occasionally, on the little money the man had, they would go to the cinema. While watching a tepid Troy Donahue film, Mark left the cinema and walked across London back to Cheyne Walk.

Derek was astonished to see him, although he admitted he knew Mark had left the hospital.

"I didn't want the LSD treatment," Mark said. "I saw on the ward what it did to people's minds. It's a crazy treatment for the crazy."

He thought he had made a joke, but Derek did not laugh.

"You'd better stay here for a while," Derek said, "but only temporarily."

Mark was given the spare room, or rather the room that no one ever slept in. It was filled with discarded objects and piles of papers. In a corner of the room there was a cot-like bed that he could sleep on. He had his meals with Derek, and Derek was polite but essentially cold to him. He knew Derek felt a sort of loathing towards him, as if he were soiled or disfigured.

"I'm going to help you," Derek said, "one last time."

"Thank you."

"I have found other accommodation for you."

In his last night in Cheyne Walk, in the room of cast-off things, Mark cried and cried, and felt that he was broken now, forever.

Cheyne Walk,
February 3rd, 1961

Dear Mr Dean,

I have arranged for Mark to be taken in by Mrs Harrison at one of the three houses which comprise her students' hostel. Provided he returns to work, he will be able to afford to live in those highly suitable surroundings at £4-15-0d per week which includes breakfast and an evening meal. He will, however, continue to need some financial help from you.

Mark moves to Mrs Harrison's on Monday February 6th, and as soon as he does so, I cannot accept any further responsibility for him, nor can I in any circumstances accommodate him again here.

In addition to this, I cannot undertake to extricate him from any financial predicament in which he may land himself – as it is I have paid out money on his behalf which I have little hope of seeing again.

I must warn you that if there is a gap between now and Mark's return to the shop, such that he cannot, without additional assistance afford to pay for his accommodation at Mrs Harrison's, and if you do not offer Mrs Harrison some guarantee of payment, and she is obliged to reject him, the situation may become dangerous for Mark who will then be at a loose end, which is very bad for him, and may land him in grave trouble.

I'm not interested in what you think about my attitude to Mark; the facts are that I have been virtually forced to accommodate him here against my will, and after he left the doctor and the hospital, I had practically no choice but to put him up here. You know as well as I do that anything he says about the matter is likely to be a complete distortion of the truth.

I have been concerned from the very first, simply and

solely with Mark's improvement and advancement in his work, and the sentimental feelings which he developed towards me were quite unexpected and unwanted.

Now that I have found him a suitable place to live, which I recommend you as his father to visit, it is up to him to make his own way.

Yours sincerely,

Derek Hadlam.

PS: Mrs Harrison's address is: ...

At the age of 67, Mark found Derek's letter among a bundle of letters from his father. His father must have sent it to him, but he had forgotten it. After reading it, he tore it up and then returned the other letters to that place in the attic where they had been for so long.

It is a long time ago. I can no longer remember the weather in the streets, or exactly what fashions we wore. Neither can I remember the opening date of *L'Avventura*. I have narrated this story. I am Mark Dean.

THE GOLDEN PRESENT

It was a warm day in April. The year was 1977. Adrian was twenty-five and this, the eighth day of the month, was his birthday. His ground floor flat in Kemp Town was filled with cards and he was spending the afternoon before his evening party alone, making sure the flat was ready. Not all of the friends who had sent cards had been invited. He had been selective, choosing those he thought were closest to him, and who loved him the most. It was important that he was loved and, more important still, that they should be there on the day of his twenty-fifth birthday.

"I will be twenty-six this time next year," he said to himself. "I will have to put away my youth and kill what remains of the adolescent in me."

He looked at the neat and tidy living room with a sense of pride. He had done his utmost to make it look its best. There were fresh flowers on the sideboard and on the table; he had bought them himself from his favourite florist. He told himself he was prepared to say goodbye to his early manhood, and that in this year of being a responsible twenty-five year old, he would do everything to put aside the follies of his past.

"No more addiction to clubs," he said to himself. "No more useless relationships. Time for a real one."

A mirror at the end of the room, which faced the long French windows that opened onto an enclosed patio, called to him. The room looked perfect, and now it was time for him to check that he looked as good himself. He told himself he was no narcissus, but it was important there were no imperfections he could not change. To add to the ridiculous solemnity of the moment he put on a recording of Elgar's *Enigma Variations*. Mentally prepared, he put an elegant foot forward and stared at his reflection. His face looked freshly back at him. It had been washed thoroughly, and his fair hair had been well shampooed. He had combed it well, untangling any unruly curls. As for his bright blue eyes, they shone brightly back at him. He had washed them carefully with a tissue, wet with lukewarm water, knowing that this helped them sparkle. His skin was tight against the bone. The more he looked, the more he was satisfied. Of course he had to let go of his adolescent years that had led so carelessly on into his twenties, but the more he looked, the more he thought, not yet, not yet. The balanced melancholy of the music in the background contradicted this with its maturity, and tired of it, he turned it off.

It was now nearly six o'clock, and time to prepare the few refreshments he was going to give his friends that evening.

"I must remember that Duncan doesn't like anything with meat in it," he said, then went into the house and made three platefuls of snacks. Finished at last, he put them on small side-tables, sat down on the sofa and waited for the doorbell to ring.

Promptly at seven, it did. A tall, lanky young man stood on the doorstep with a bottle of wine in his hand. His name was Nicholas. He was an up-and-coming conductor.

"I hope this is alright," he said awkwardly and handed the bottle to Adrian. "I'm not very good on wines."

Adrian took the wine and noted that it was not an especially good one, but then he reminded himself that Nicholas led a spartan life in a large spartan house in Hove and dismissed the crude sensations of the flesh—the category into which his dry taste of life put the invigorating but useless taste of wine.

"I am sure it is perfect," Adrian said politely, and stood aside so Nicholas could enter the flat.

"The first to arrive." Nicholas smiled his boyish smile and stood in the centre of the room, all arms and legs, and with a smile that made Adrian think of a newly born, rather unstable horse.

"Where shall I sit?" Nicholas asked.

Before Adrian could answer, he saw that Nicholas had found the most uncomfortable chair in the room: a tall, high-backed black chair that had been bought rashly from an antiques dealer in Lewes.

"You can't possibly be comfortable," Adrian said.

"We don't all need comforts like you," Nicholas replied. "I grew up in a country manor that had nothing but chairs like this. My father thought it was good for the body. Anyway, that's how he put it. Not like you in your family's Buckinghamshire mansion with all that money to indulge yourself."

Nicholas had a sharp way of putting things. He called them truthful things, and as much as Adrian loved him, he hated him for it.

"My aunt left me enough to buy this flat, not my parents. They're still alive and living in Amersham."

"It comes to the same thing, doesn't it?"

Nicholas smiled as he said this and with a long arm, reached out for the recording of the *Enigma Variations* which lay abandoned on the floor.

"Music for the deaf," he said.

"You sound as if Adorno, or whoever it is that you read, would not approve of this music."

Nicholas gave a little snort of sound, and then placed the recording back onto the floor. He smiled at Adrian and said, "You'd better be careful, or someone will step on it."

"I have some Stockhausen," Adrian said. "Would you like me to put that on?"

"I can't imagine who gave it to you," Nicholas mumbled. "You certainly didn't go out and buy it."

"It doesn't matter either way. Would you like to hear it?"

"What's it called?"

"I can't remember. Something to do with light I think. It's over there with the others. But please, if you do, play it only until the others arrive."

Nicholas laughed his dry laugh.

"Do I know them?"

"I'm not sure. There's Duncan, the writer, with his friend who is a painter.

"I think I met Duncan once or maybe twice. Rather fat and camp. Always dressed in clashing colours. Has a low opinion of his own sexuality."

"If that's your interpretation of Duncan, then that is Duncan. But don't you equally have opinions?"

"It's different," Nicholas said vaguely, and reached over for a snack. It was a piece of cheese on a cracker. On top of the cheese, impaled, was an olive. Also on the plate were some rather slimy looking anchovies. He reached out awkwardly and the plate with all its contents fell to the floor.

"Oh, hell!" he said.

"Never mind. I'll do it."

"I'm not usually this awkward."

They were both now on the floor, salvaging the scattered food and putting it back onto the plate. Nicholas blew on the snacks to get rid of a few specks of dust. Adrian looked appalled.

"I can remember you always being very awkward," he said.

"Can you?

"Yes. That first time we went to bed in that hotel room in Dieppe. We were both a little drunk and on our way to Paris."

"I was eighteen. Of course I was awkward. You were a year older and should have been more patient with me."

"There are certain messes one cannot clean up," Adrian said. "Sex between individuals who are not really attracted to each other is one of them."

"You fancied me," Nicholas replied, stuffing the last of the fallen snacks into his mouth. "It was I who didn't fancy you."

Before this conversation could go any further, the bell rang. Adrian ran to the door.

"Duncan."

And there he was, brighter and much larger than the unusually hot but fading April day. His hair was a blond tangle, and the bloom on his rounded cheeks flushed deeply. He had a big parcel in his hands and pushed it almost aggressively into Adrian's arms.

"Dearest one," he gushed, "it's a lamp. I'm telling you that now so you don't have to tell the truth when you tell me you like it."

"But Duncan, you are alone." Adrian took the parcel and looked expectantly behind him. "Where is Arthur?" he asked.

"Arthur had to finish off a painting. Urgently. You know what it is to hover on the brink of losing inspiration. He said you would understand, and that if he has it finished in time he will come on later."

He noticed Nicholas and waved.

"Hello," he said in a long drawn out tone. Pushing past Adrian, he went into the room and reached out for Nicholas's hand.

"I heard about your first concert," he said. "I heard it was absolutely marvellous. Mahler's Fourth. How ambitious. Was the singer right in the last movement? Was she the person you wanted?"

Nicholas shuffled his feet and Adrian could see he was hating this encounter and above all, this questioning.

"It wasn't all that good," he mumbled.

"But the critics, my dear. I read the critics. It said how promising you were. Didn't they say you should try to record a cycle?"

"Yes."

"Well then, you must. You absolutely must. Mahler is *the* thing at the moment. No one else to listen to really. Not in my book anyway. He's got so much more expansion than anyone else. I can't think of another composer I like better."

"I can," Nicholas replied sourly and then rather rudely turned his back on him.

"Who else is coming?" Duncan asked and turned to Adrian.

"Nicholas was asking that just before you arrived," he lied.

"Well, tell me, tell me."

He plumped himself down on the sofa, and taking up a large part of it, began to eat the snacks on the side table next to him.

"I'd beware of those," Nicholas said. "They've been on the floor."

"Oh, don't be so silly," Duncan said, glaring at Nicholas, then filled his mouth with anchovy. He hated meat, but loved fish and damn it all, he was determined to eat them all. If Adrian could have read his mind he would have heard him ask why couldn't he have prepared them all some delicious, large, vegetarian (save for the fish) meal.

"Anyway," he said as he munched, "tell me all. Tell me who else is coming."

"A woman friend who works in a religious bookshop. Spare time of course. She doesn't need the money, but she does like religion."

"How absolutely fascinating," Duncan said. "It's not one of those awful esoteric shops, is it?"

Nicholas guffawed loudly. Duncan turned and glared at him again.

"I mean, is it one of those shops where they peddle all those alternative religions? Zen and all that? Being a lapsed Catholic, I wouldn't approve."

"It caters for all western religions," Adrian replied. "It is a very ordinary bookshop."

"Oh," he said and then waved a hand in the air as if dismissing any further talk on the subject.

Adrian knew that Duncan didn't much like women either.

"But there must be other people," Duncan added. "Some of your more wicked friends from the clubs and pubs. I haven't met any of them. Surely on this special day you won't keep them all hidden away. And isn't there one you really like?

Being *married* to Arthur, I don't go to clubs anymore."

Adrian put on his ambiguous smile, realising only too well that once Duncan had enough alcohol in him, he was always ready to listen to him tell of his sexual conquests. This had been a continuing ritual throughout the years of their friendship. When they were alone together, first it was talk about the failure of most homosexuals and how they couldn't sustain relationships (except Duncan and Arthur of course), and then in total contradiction, demands for more earthy details of promiscuity and the flesh. At that time, for someone of Duncan's generation, being in his early fifties, homosexuality always had to be talked of with some sort of implicit shame: shame expressed with comments like, *well, they don't last, do they, relationships like ours? Be honest, darling, this awful word 'gay' has made it all so tawdry. We are not gay, we are queer. We always will be. Normals will never accept us.* He knew Duncan well, and his prejudices, and as a friend does, tolerated him and loved him despite them. So, the ambiguous smile he gave Duncan, tantalised him. He could see it. He was clearly waiting for *the* guest to arrive. Adrian could almost hear Duncan's voice ring out, "Who is he?" So to prevent him from being so crass he jumped in immediately with what he wanted to hear.

"His name is Claude."

"Claude!"

Duncan clapped his hands together in delight.

"You met him in a club? Do tell."

"No darling, I met him in a small French restaurant nearby."

"Was he eating alone?"

"Actually no. He was one of the waiters."

"Well!"

His response was long and protracted, and Nicholas who had returned to his puritan chair had a fit of the giggles.

"Is he lonely?" Duncan continued. "You always love those lonely, pretty boys. And he must be intelligent as well. After all, how could you possibly not want to share the knowledge you have of beautiful antiques and paintings and music? He must have it all. I know it."

"Do you?" Nicholas's voice rang out like a bell.

"What do you mean by that remark?" Duncan turned on Nicholas with a frown. All the bouncy inflections in his voice had gone. He sounded as hard as stone, and the tone of his question had in it all the defiance of a call for battle. Who was this worm? This worm of a conductor who was Adrian's other best friend? Who was he to constantly mock him when he was so dried up and constipated himself? Had he ever looked at a vivid orange Van Gogh sunflower painting and loved it? Had he ever listened to the lush sounds of Szymanowski and wallowed in it? In fact, had he ever lived at all?

"Well?" he insisted.

"I know Adrian's tastes perhaps better than you do," Nicholas replied, feigning politeness. His mouth was one big smile as he spoke. "Adrian may love Mahler and all things beautiful, but when it comes down to, how shall I put it, bodily parts, his tastes are more mundane. There, he is all flesh, and lots of it. As I believe you are a vegetarian, I realise this may be hard to take, but when Adrian eats of the flesh, he eats it right down to the bone."

Duncan sniffed loudly, then teasing his blond tangle of hair, curled himself closer into the sofa and with the slightest hint of mockery followed his sniff with a loud yawn.

The bell saved them all. Adrian leapt to the door as if it were his salvation. He hoped to see the last, the dearest last peccadillo of his advanced adolescence on the doorstep. He opened the door with a silent prayer that begged for a lingering twenty-fifth year in which to enjoy his adolescent capacity for loving.

"Jenny," he said, hiding his disappointment as best he could. She stood in front of him, trim and charmingly beautiful. In her hand, she held a present that by its shape he knew to be a book.

"Am I very late?" she asked.

"No. No. Our small party is just beginning."

She came in and knowing neither of the people in front of her, just stood there and glowed goodness at them. In Jenny there was no evil, nor did she see any. Yet Adrian knew she was only too aware that evil existed.

"Jenny, meet my friends Nicholas and Duncan."

Nicholas stood and shook hands. Duncan remained on his sofa, defiantly expanding himself on it so that no one like Jenny or Nicholas could sit down beside him.

"Isn't it time to pour the wine?" Duncan asked languidly.

Adrian did the honours and for the next hour, time plus two bottles of wine, passed between them all. Duncan drank the most, with Adrian a close second. Nicholas sipped at his rather cautiously, and Jenny dipped her head at the glass like a shy bird. Then, at precisely a quarter to ten, the doorbell rang again. No longer so eager to answer, Adrian opened the door and a good looking, if rather ordinary young man stood on the doorstep.

"I am inexcusably past the time," he said in bad English.

"Is that Claude?" Duncan boomed.

"Do I know this man?" Claude asked.

"Come in and meet my friends," Adrian said.

Like dancers rehearsing steps they both knew and did not know, the rituals of meeting this foreign young man were gone through. Duncan waved like a big sodden plant in the wind. Jenny was polite and a little confused, while Nicholas appraised him silently and with pleasure. Adrian could see that behind his brittle, professional mask, Nicholas approved.

"He's very young."

Duncan meant to whisper, but it was as loud as a prompt reminding a flustered actor of a forgotten line. Claude heard it and blushed. He had seated himself in a chair next to Jenny and Adrian noticed with irony that they made a handsome couple.

"Let's have some music," Duncan said. It was an order,

and not a request. "Some Richard Strauss. I like Richard Strauss. You've got him, haven't you Adrian?"

Adrian smiled and after a few silent minutes, put on the last act of *Der Rosenkavalier*.

"Ah, that is so, so beautiful," Duncan said, and drank deeply from his cup of dark wine.

"Fascist nonsense," Nicholas said loudly. "All that cacophony of oh so profound meaning. I wonder he didn't strangle himself in the terrible web of his own notes." He then turned to the others and asked if anyone else knew or liked Richard Strauss.

"I prefer Bach," Jenny said simply. Then she added, and it sounded a little perverse coming from her so beautiful and good mouth, "With Strauss I can also hear the jackboots marching."

"Strauss was above politics," Duncan said. "Above all that social rigmarole. He was—" and here he floundered.

"Transcendent?" Nicholas mocked.

"Yes. Precisely yes."

Duncan gesticulated so vigorously that the wine in his glass spilled over the sofa. Adrian looked and cursed mentally at this stain on his birthday.

"What about you, Claude?" Duncan asked, turning on him. "Do you have an opinion?"

"I don't know much music *classique*," came the humble reply.

"Pop, is it?" Duncan asked.

At that moment Claude got up and going over to Adrian, asked if they could go somewhere quiet to talk. The request was overheard by the others, and both Nicholas and Duncan thought that a quick bout of physical passion was in the young man's mind.

"Don't be long, my dears," Duncan called out.

Fifteen minutes of desultory conversation followed between the three who were left stranded in the living room. Not one of them had anything in common with the others.

Duncan looked at his watch and was wondering if it was best to call it a day, when Adrian and Claude returned.

"I hope you may understand," Claude said politely to Adrian.

Adrian was fighting back tears and bit on his lower lip. Nicholas saw at once that something was wrong and went up to him. To avoid even the briefest of explanations, Adrian moved away and sat beside Jenny. She looked at him and smiled, and with a feeling of helplessness he wanted her to hold him in her arms.

"I have to go," Claude said, loudly and awkwardly.

A look passed briefly between all of them, and then, as if he had never been there at all, Claude was gone. The highlight of the evening had not delivered its fireworks.

Duncan heaved himself off the sofa and asked in a very loud voice what was the matter.

"His girlfriend is waiting for him," Adrian said at last.

Duncan let out a coarse laugh.

"So that's it," he said. "Another of *them*. Aren't most of the boys you choose like that? I've always said so, haven't I?"

"Like what?" Jenny asked with a certain amount of innocence.

"Oh, these semi-queers—always running off to get married. Normality always calls them in the end. But it's been a good evening. Lots of lovely music, wine and talk." He turned to Adrian and said rather callously, "Well, you didn't really need him, did you?"

He was ready to go, and Adrian showed him the door. When he had left, Nicholas said, "Thank God for that," and repeated more or less the same thing as Duncan had said, "If a young man is undecided and decides to do the normal thing, well, there is little that anyone can or should do." His final words were simply that Adrian should accept it and get on with his life.

The door closed behind him. Only Jenny remained.

"Did you love him?" She asked this very quietly and

looked down as if shy at having had to ask this question. If it was love, it was good, and that was all that mattered to her.

"I was not quite there," Adrian replied. "But yes, let us call it love."

Jenny looked around the room, and then out of the long windows into the night.

"You have a beautiful home," she said, "and it is your birthday. In a year's time you will have another birthday, and it may all be better by then."

"Yes," Adrian said mechanically and sat down on the sofa directly on the wet spot where Duncan had spilled his wine.

"You are younger than me, Jenny, but much wiser. That's why I love you so much as a friend. Do they get better, as you get older? Birthdays I mean?"

"It's a cliché, Adrian, but you have the whole of your life in front of you. Yes, I think the birthdays do get better. Take my father for instance. He was a child until he was forty, and on each birthday he would cry like a child, and do you know why he cried? The golden present hadn't come." She paused, then added, "That's what he always called his birthday—the golden present to come. And with each birthday, it failed to arrive. Of course I don't remember this. My mother told me. But I can believe it. He was restless, and yes, totally self-absorbed. The golden present was his by right and he expected too much. Then quite suddenly, when forty came, he was quiet. He accepted."

She stood up and going over to the sofa, reached down to take Adrian's hand.

"One day, you will accept as well. You will accept the day as it is. One step further along the path."

"To what?" Adrian asked.

"Maybe to the golden present that will come after all, once it is not expected, and by being not expected, able to be received."

Adrian smiled at her in some sort of disbelief. Where would he be when he was forty?

HOME

"But my dear, you sound as if you blame us."

Eric faced them. He sat in the smallest chair in the room with a tea cup held unsteadily in his hand.

"I don't blame anybody," he said slowly.

"We did everything in our power at the time to persuade you not to go."

The small chorus clucked their approval in front of him. He heard one voice ask for a second cup of tea and a third ask for another slice of delicious cake. In a far corner of the room an old Edwardian clock chimed the hour. Five o'clock. He had been in the room for an hour.

"It was my choice. I had to go. I had to leave here. I had no friends—"

The chorus let out a collective gasp. In this statement he had reproached them for not being there.

"Of course you had friends."

The voice that said the words poured him another cup of tea. His hand felt so shaky that the tea almost poured over his trousers. He drank the tea down quickly, then said that he must go.

"As you wish."

The voice was brisk, and when he stood up he was shown silently and firmly to the door.

"Eric, it's always difficult coming back."

He mumbled something in return. It may have been no, it may have been yes. Once outside the big house on The Drive he walked quickly, making his way to the comfort of the sea.

"I must not be angry," he said aloud to himself. "I must not blame. It is the worst thing I can do."

Reaching the seafront he made his way towards Brighton.

He walked the length of Hove Lawns, past the angel that had once marked the boundary dividing Brighton from Hove and looked with tired eyes upon a view that he had once loved but now barely knew: the shock of the West Pier's skeletal remains in the sea always hit him like a personal loss.

"They could have saved it," he said to himself. "They could have prevented it from happening. No one was really there for that pier. It was once so popular and then for no fault of its own, abandoned. From that moment on, it was left to its decay and its destruction."

He had not been there when the final *Götterdämmerung* had happened: when the last flames had burned off all the flesh of memory from its bones. He had seen pictures of course, and he had heard rumours of why it may have happened and how, but there was still a secret about its death, and at the core of this secret they had wished upon it a dreadful posterity. They had made the twisted skeleton into an icon. It was now a permanent reminder of Brighton's lost beauty surrounded by an architectural chorus of fading Regency squares and badly kept houses.

"This is how it ends," he said, and looked out at the reddened structural remnants, forever scalded by the heat of its final hours.

"A crematorium in the sea," he whispered, then moved on.

He walked for hours that summer's evening, not wanting to return to his newly acquired room. He walked eastwards, out to the Marina and from there looked towards Rottingdean.

"I must go there," he said, and tired though he was he walked half way. He wanted to see the Burne-Jones windows in their church setting. He wanted to see with his failing eyes a blaze of colour that he hoped would never be destroyed. Then he realised that at this hour the church would be closed.

"If I could start all over again," he said, "I would make my home there. Why is it, when we are young, we never realise we have the nearest thing to paradise on our doorstep?"

He was talking aloud in the open space that separated the

downs from the sea, standing on the brink of a cliff. A momentary thought of suicide entered his mind. I could climb over, he thought, then just let myself go in free fall. I'm in free fall already, so why not make an end to it? But knowing he was a coward made him step back from the brink.

"I must go on until it ends," he said aloud. "I must let it all go onwards to its natural conclusion."

Chastising himself now for over-indulging in self-pity he turned round and retraced his steps back into the heart of Brighton. Darkness had almost fallen. The lights were coming on.

"I am hungry," he said aloud. "How I wish—"

He lowered his head, shut his mouth and said nothing more. He did not even want to finish the sentence in his mind. He did not want to wish for either the departed or the dead to be waiting for him in his room. He was old and he was tired, but he preferred to be alone to eat his dinner.

Only the dingy room in Clarence Square was waiting for him. It was on the top floor and thankfully from the window he had a view of the trees in the square. The walls were a dusty green: the colour of grass when it has been walked over by too many muddy shoes. As for furniture, he had a single bed that had less life in it than he, a table that was scarred with too much use, and a cracked washbasin in the corner. The only feature of interest to someone coming into the room, other than himself, was a reproduction of a minor Victorian painter that hung above the bed. It was a sentimental scene: a cosy little house with a happy looking heterosexual couple warming themselves before a blazing fire. The only thing the picture did for him was to remind him to turn on the small freestanding electric fire.

"Home," he said sarcastically and sat down on the bed. In the inventory of things in the room he always forgot, were the sagging green chairs, equal in their ugliness to the colour of the walls. He also forgot the ruin of a two-ring cooker and the brown splodge of a sideboard that it stood on.

"Time for dinner," he said.

He opened a drawer in the sideboard and took out a tin opener. Below that in a cupboard he had his food. Tins of Tuna wobbled uneasily on top of each other. He took one out, followed by a pathetically small tin of potatoes. He then reached for the last of a group of shrivelled tomatoes that had been sitting in a cracked glass bowl for a week.

"This should keep me alive," he said.

Sitting at the table after he had finished eating, he did what he always did night after night since he had started renting the room. He wondered to himself how he had got there, and like a recording on constant replay, he replayed the past that had led him to this point in his life.

Krapp's Last Tape, he called it in remembrance of Samuel Beckett, and the theatre, and of plays he had once loved.

"I was an actor."

He said this every night, aloud and proud, as if it confirmed the essence of his existence.

"I was good in Beckett," he said. "I excelled in Beckett. Now I am living like a character out of Beckett."

These words always gave him a certain dismal comfort. They were like a mantra that seemed to objectify and in some way justify what he saw as the failure of his existence.

"I am seventy-two years old, and I was an actor."

He would then recite remembered words, words fished out of his mind to parade once more before him. The dismal room took on the proportions of a stage. And there he was, the single being in the spotlight of his memory, speaking the words and walking the floor, conscious that he was the focus of attention, conscious that he was not alone, and that he had a crowd of people looking at him in rapt attention and very often in admiration.

But tonight, this night, the conjuring up of his temporary success did not succeed. He remembered that other small crowd, the crowd in the room that afternoon, who had sneered and not so discretely jeered at his return to Brighton.

His mind went back fifteen years. He had a small flat in the centre of Brighton which he owned and he was grieving for a friend who had died of AIDS.

"You must come round whenever you like."

One of the chorus of his acquaintances had said this in the street a few weeks after his friend's death.

"Eric, you know you are always welcome. Is it just a natural reticence that keeps you away from us?"

He had taken the invitation seriously. He had called the number he thought he could trust, but was met by an answering machine.

"I am sorry, but there is no one home at the moment. If you would like to leave your name and number I will get back to you as soon as possible."

He persisted in calling until one Saturday morning he got through. In the background he could hear retro music from the seventies.

"It's Eric."

"At last." The words were said breathily, as if long lost news had finally arrived.

"I rang several times. Always the answering machine."

"Oh my dear, it has a fault. I forgot to tell you. The wretched thing must be changed. The messages will just not record. Oh dear, I am so sorry."

"But you are never in."

"Of course I am in. Often in. Is it my fault if you call when I am out?"

"I called several times. More times than I should have, I felt as if I was pestering."

"How could you be pestering? You are one of the people I respect and admire the most. How good you were in that absurd play called—what was it called? *Rhinoceros*? I am sure I have got that wrong."

"Ionesco."

"Oh, was it?"

"Ionesco's *Rhinoceros*."

"Absurd title. Absurd name. But you were superb. You held the play if I remember. We all said that you did."

"That was a long time ago."

"Time passes, dear. We are not all in our first flush anymore, are we?"

This was followed by a long silence.

"I was wondering if I could come round for a talk. Maybe in the next few days."

Another very long silence.

"Eric, I would love it, but you have caught me on the hop. I am surrounded by two large suitcases and a few helpers who are getting really exasperated with me. I am going away for a while. A much nicer stretch of water than the English Channel calls me. I am off to Capri and the temporary comfort of a rented villa. Oh dear, I suppose I should have told you this was on the horizon when we met. But please, please, please call when I get back."

A few more words were exchanged, and then the line went dead. Eric tried a few more numbers and a few more 'friends' who had disappeared off the map when his friend had died, but all were either indisposed (unspecified illnesses) or on the point of going out to an important dinner or a concert or theatre event they could not possibly miss.

"I am sorry I rang."

He found he was saying this over and over again. Eventually he got the message that everyone he knew was unavailable and he shut his door. He consoled himself with the fact that he had a good flat. He even had an open fire which gave a semblance of comfort. And for months the comfort did last. He read Dickens until he had exhausted Dickens, which is in itself a feat. Then he turned to George Eliot. He could have gone on to a quiz programme with all the knowledge he had acquired about these two authors. He also drank too much, and in the hours between his immersion in Victorian novels he indulged himself in the company of very late twentieth century rent boys. He saved monthly for the privilege.

Then one day in early spring he stared at his late fifties face in the mirror and decided that the walls were closing in. He rang acquaintance number one who had been back for a long time from Capri but was still unavailable to be seen, and told him what he intended to do.

"I am going to sell the flat," he said.

"Sell it? My dear, you are crazy. Nothing, nothing equals property."

"But I want to go away. I want to be somewhere else."

"I am sure there is nowhere else quite like Brighton. And anyway, what about your acting?"

"I haven't been asked to play a role for a long time."

"It's because you're not talking to the right people. I've always thought this about you. You have always insisted on being in such obscure plays. I mean, I don't want to offend, but most of the crowd I know only went along because they knew you were in them. I mean, you must have been asked to play in a Rattigan or a Coward."

"Yes."

"And?"

"I wasn't suited to Rattigan or Coward."

"Well, there are others. Only the other year there was a spate of revivals of delightful 1950s comedies. The Theatre Royal alone was littered with them. You surely could have put yourself up for one of those. If nothing else I have contacts. You could have asked me."

"My friend was very ill at the time. Those revivals came at the time when he was in and out of hospital."

"Oh my dear, of course. I always forget. But in between hospital visits and all that, you could have kept going with some minor part to keep your name alive."

"I chose not to do that."

A long silence.

"We all have our crosses to bear."

The heavy sigh on the end of the phone signalled to Eric

that he was overstaying his telephone welcome and that it was time to cut to the chase.

"So where do you want to go?"

The voice sounded impatient. Eric imagined a much needed drink near at hand, or perhaps a more amusing companion than himself.

"Amsterdam."

He could almost hear the splash as the stone fell into the amazed pond.

"Amsterdam!"

The water sprayed all over him.

"Yes. I want a challenge. A new language."

"But my dear, Dutch is not a language. No one speaks it. Or maybe they do between grunts and groans in a dustbin in a Beckett play."

"All the same, I want to go there."

"Do you know the place?"

He explained that he had been there with his friend several times and that they had liked it very much. He had even said to his friend that he would like to go and live in the city. To which his friend, who knew he was dying, had smiled and said simply that he wished him well.

"I must say I admire your courage."

The words came at him down the phone like dialogue retrieved from a very old film.

"I just feel so alone here."

The naked words had been said to which of course there could be no real reply. All he heard was a coughing sound and further away, turned down, the incessant beat of 1970s disco music.

"I think you should think about it, and if I wasn't so busy at the moment I would talk to you about this in more depth."

"Thank you for listening."

He put down the phone, and that night dreamed that he was living in a nice canal house in the heart of old Amsterdam. In his dream he was surrounded by new friends and also lots of amazingly good looking blond boys. In the morning he put his flat up for sale and took the first flight he could to Schiphol. It was during that stay that he found his first rather ugly flat on the outskirts of Amsterdam and heard from the estate agent that he had had an offer on his Brighton flat. He accepted the offer and within months he was no longer a resident of England, but alone and adrift in Amsterdam.

At first it had been exciting. He had plenty of money in the bank to live on and used it lavishly on rent boys and acquaintances met in bars, but he never got around to learning the language because he found he had no aptitude for languages. Then, before he knew what was happening, the boom in house prices in England had begun, and just when he decided he had had enough of wasting his life in Amsterdam he realised he could not afford to return to England.

"You could have told me prices were soaring."

He said this during one of his infrequent calls to acquaintance number one in Brighton.

"My dear it just happened. I hardly knew myself. Of course we're all delighted that our own properties have risen in value so much, but poor you! If I had only known you hadn't been sensible enough to buy something there, I would have been in touch at once."

"Would you?" he asked disbelievingly.

"Eric, you're not accusing me of keeping something from you, are you?"

He replied that he was not accusing him at all.

"I mean, it's not my fault if you cannot now afford to buy even a broom cupboard."

"Do you know of any broom cupboards I could afford?" he had replied sarcastically.

"I can tell you are upset with the world, but really darling, you did make this decision in full awareness of what you were doing. I know it was probably grief dictating your actions, but grief shouldn't do that."

"What should it do?" he asked.

"You come number one in your life. A friend dies, tragically if I may say so, but your life goes on."

A pause.

"But instead of letting it go on in one place, you chose to hop abroad to Europe. As I said at the time, it may have taken a sort of great courage, but now you probably see that it was just a little bit foolish."

He said that he knew acquaintance number one was always right as usual and after a few false pleasantries the phone was mutually put down.

He stayed on in Amsterdam, living on a decreased income and slowly descending down the moral ladder. He chose his company badly and soon was cruelly and often reminded that he was an old man. His body began to give up on him and he had to take a revolting liquid that tasted like soup, to make his digestion work every morning. His eyesight deteriorated and he suspected there were deeper and more serious health problems. It was during his fourteenth year away from England that he met a very inexpensive rent boy who said he knew a friend of a friend who had a house in Brighton with rooms to rent.

"I do want to go home," he said.

The rent boy looked at him with some sort of automatic pity and said he would ring his friend.

"Could you do it now?" Eric had asked.

The boy requested some money to cover the call and having taken more than was necessary, rang his friend.

"I've got a guy here who's in trouble, and he needs a room in Brighton." He turned to Eric and asked, "How old are you?"

"In my fifties."

"Come on, the truth."

"Seventy."

The boy gave a sigh, and turned back to the mobile phone.

"He says he is seventy."

He then laughed and said, "Well, he won't mind then, will he?"

"What's he asking?"

The boy covered the phone with his hand and said, "The place is a tip. It's in pretty bad shape. Even the students don't want it."

"Anything."

The boy spoke into the phone.

"He'll take it. It's how much?"

The room was cheap, and within the month he had managed to leave the run-down block of flats in south-east Amsterdam.

Of course, he hated the room. Of course, he knew he could look around for better but, aside from the fact that he was only entitled to the very lowest of benefits, a sort of despair had set in: a drift inwards to his most secret self where he no longer really cared what the future held. Then one day he rang acquaintance number one to say he was back.

"My dear, I couldn't be more surprised. You really must come over for tea."

It was as if the door to Kafka's castle had opened.

"Do you want me to ring again to fix a date?"

"No, no, come tomorrow. We will have a little celebration. Just a few old people to welcome you back."

He went round to the house on The Drive where they were all assembled. A small group of faces that smirked when they smiled, and a few jokes made about the price to be paid for a boy in Amsterdam.

"Now don't go pretending that you don't know the price," acquaintance number one had said.

"And where are you living now?" a voice he did not recognise asked.

"Clarence Square."

"My dear, you have fallen on your feet. It's so central. But really, I know it's not as nice as it used to be when we were young, is it? All those dreadful students with all their money—and the parties! I know I couldn't live there with all that noise. Hove is, well, Hove."

He sipped his tea and then quite suddenly he came out with the words, "I should have been told. I should have been told it was all getting too expensive. Those dreadful prices going up. Soaring up and leaving me stranded, and no one telling me."

"We all thought you were so settled."

Acquaintance number one sat rigidly in his chair and poured tea with increasing nervous regularity.

"No one rang me. No one wrote to me."

"Did we have an address? Did we have a number?"

The question went round the room like a tiny flame, burning them all just a little with a hint of reproach. A small tidal wave of no's came back and settled on the uneasy shore of the afternoon. It was then that acquaintance number one said, "But my dear, you sound as if you blame us."

DESCENT OF ANGELS

It was a cold, early January evening in New York. I had just eaten a pizza at a restaurant in the Upper East Side. Across from my table a solitary man had been staring at me as I ate my meal. He was around my age—in his late fifties— and while I was drinking coffee he raised his glass of wine and smiled at me. I had no desire to meet him and decided to pay and leave. Inwardly I felt angry and irritable as I had intended to stay a while longer in the restaurant and just reflect on the events of the previous year. I was getting old and wanted to take stock and not to be disturbed. I called the waiter over and asked him to bend down so I could whisper into his ear. He knew me well as a regular and obliged. I asked who the man was who had been, and was still, staring at me. He whispered back that the man's name was Floyd Barclay and that although he had not seen him for several years, he had been a regular like me, and then had just stopped coming. I asked the waiter if he could ask him either to stop staring or to come over to my table. The waiter questioned whether he should wait until the man had finished his pizza. I said no. Enough was enough. I had decided now to stay. I wasn't often looked at any more and I was curious. I would ask him what he wanted. The waiter straightened up and looked at me, trying to hide his embarrassment at such a request, but nodded his head, gave me a wan smile, and I watched as he went over to the man's table. In imitation to what he had done for me I saw him bend down and whisper in the man's ear. The man smiled, looked over at me and got up from his table at once. The waiter scurried away, as if to say, let them get on with it.

Floyd Barclay crossed the space that divided us and sat

down opposite me at my table.

"Good pizza here," he said with a smile.

"I come here once a week," I said flatly. "I like it."

"I'm Floyd Barclay."

He held out his hand, but rudely I refused to take it or give him my name.

"I suppose you are angry that I have been staring at you," he said simply. "You come here to be alone and quiet and here I am, a rude and pushy stranger."

"You did stare all the time I was eating," I said petulantly.

"Yes. I apologise. Or rather, I should say, it got me to my objective."

"Which is?"

"To get to know you."

I laughed and raised my coffee cup to my lips. I drank the last drop down to the dregs. When I had lowered the cup to the plate I looked hard at him.

"It can't be for my stunning looks," I said.

"You shouldn't underestimate yourself. You are still a very attractive man. Your kind of looks don't die when most people's looks die."

I laughed again, for at that moment I knew he had caught my attention. I was no longer angry and no longer felt the desire to be rude to him. He was flattering me after all and that hadn't happened in a long time.

"My name is Michael Field," I said offering him my hand across the table, and like an old-fashioned character in an even older film he stood up, and reaching across the table shook my hand. After that he sat down.

"I owe you an explanation," he said.

"No. Let's keep the mystery going a while longer. I only stayed longer in this restaurant out of curiosity. I saw you drinking wine. Shall I order a bottle?"

"I'll have coffee," he replied and looked briefly at my empty cup. "Black and strong, like yours."

The waiter took our order and smiled at us both as if he

had been a successful cupid in bringing us together.

"Well, the waiter looks pleased," Floyd observed.

"Mission accomplished," I murmured wryly, and Floyd laughed softly.

For all the world, I thought, we must look like a couple. I haven't felt like a couple for a very long time.

"What's your line of business, Floyd?" I asked.

"Show business."

"Glamourous," I said.

"Was. Most of my clients are dead, or in the process of dying. I'm still an agent, but at this rate I will retire in a year or two. Do you remember Gracie Marshall?"

I said that I had not heard of her.

"She made a comeback in the sixties. You know, small roles on Broadway. Well, she died earlier today. Henderson Place."

"Nice address," I added.

"Messy death. She killed herself with a carving knife at the age of ninety-one. She was dying of cancer, so I don't quite understand why she couldn't have waited. Anyway, it will be small news tomorrow."

"I don't read the papers," I said.

"It was early this morning. I was out walking and saw the ambulance. A woman neighbour told me who it was and what had happened. She had keys to her place and had heard screaming."

"Even suicides don't have to like it when they actually achieve their objective."

He smiled and asked if we could change the subject.

"Just made me feel like the whole business is dying, which of course it isn't. But Gracie was with me, and I felt kind of responsible as her agent. Then I had a phone call from—"

He stopped and looked at me and in his look I saw a guilty expression that said he was saying too much.

"Well," I said, filling in the pause of the conversation, "I think you said we should change the subject. Shall we talk about the weather?"

"It's January. What can you say about January?"

"So, what made you come to this restaurant?" I asked.

"I used to come here years ago. I got a bit sentimental for a comfort I had forgotten. I even put aside a ticket for a Schütz concert tonight. His *St. Matthew Passion*."

"Very austere," I said.

"I like austere. It's better than all that bland tinkling of the ivories you hear in some of these Upper East Side apartments. In my line of business I spend a lot of time in them. There's nothing more awful than the very old reminiscing about piano players."

He sighed, looked at me as if he was going to suddenly make a declaration of love, and said, "You were at an apartment. East 94th. It was twenty-five years ago."

I laughed.

"You remember?" I asked in astonishment.

"I expect you don't."

"Well, I have been to a lot of apartments in a lot of streets in twenty-five years. That must have made it around '78."

"Right," Floyd said. "Before the paranoid era."

"You mean AIDS," I added.

"What else?"

"I didn't think you meant the World Trade Center."

"Let's not talk about that." He began to play with the unused cutlery on my table, and then without warning he came out with the words, "What made you the best hustler in New York? You know you could have been an actor. What else are actors today, but hustler lookalikes? At that gathering in East 94th I saw your potential. I could have signed you on there and then."

"Why didn't you?" I asked.

"I suppose you must have looked too happy with your then current profession." He paused and looked at me with the same stare that had begun our encounter. "You were happy, weren't you?"

"As you said, it was the seventies, and there was a lot of high-priced work out there. It's sick to say it, but there were so many more people alive then."

"No names," he said.

"Don't worry," I replied, "I wasn't going to give any."

Floyd then looked flustered and began rather absurdly to build a structure out of the napkins. I sensed he had something to say, and asked him politely to stop messing about with the things on my table.

"Alright." His hands came to rest and he gave me that hard stare again. "Michael, I want to ask you how long it has been since you gave up your—well, your work."

"If you mean my hustling, back in '85. Since then I've been running a very successful hotel near Washington Square. You can't be still interested in me for that? I mean I could consider a proposition without money, but not with. I am in my late fifties now and despite your very flattering opening lines, I cannot see myself any more in my former role. I really would not know how to play the part."

"Have you heard of Adam Wales?" he asked suddenly.

"Yes. He was killed in his apartment. When was it? Thirty years ago? Hollywood's golden boy."

"Exact."

"Well?"

"Adam Wales was not killed thirty years ago. He is alive, but not so well, living in a large apartment on 5th Avenue."

I sat back in my chair and let out a long, low whistle. He sat back in his and stared hard at me again.

"Have I taken the wind out of your sails?"

"He was my idol," I said slowly. "I mean he was everyone's idol. But no one wanted to *be* him more than me."

"You have something of his looks," Floyd added.

"More flattery. Even if I had been almost as good-looking as him, I hadn't a fraction of his talent. I mean, my God, the way he acted. The way he walked. It was all so effortless. Like Mozart. Like nothing less than perfection. No, Floyd, I have nothing and never had anything that Adam Wales had."

I closed my eyes and had a brief and very vivid waking dream. I was there in his last film. I was there down in California at the filming of that final scene of *Descent of Angels*. I was walking towards him on the set. We were surrounded by an eager crowd, ready to call it a day, and there I was, the object of his desire. The one person in the whole picture that he desired, that he was going to kiss at the fadeout. The waking dream was so vivid, I cried out.

"Are you alright?"

Floyd was at my side, steadying the chair I was sitting on. I had almost flipped it totally backwards with me on it.

"Yes," I said unsteadily.

"Water."

He made me sip out of a glass. I put it down, said I was better and he returned to his seat.

"It was the shock," I whispered. "It was the complete and total shock. I was in love with that man. I saw each of his few films, time and time again. I remember going to my favourite Greenwich Village movie theater and just sitting there for three continuous shows."

"Then I can tell him you're a fan?" Floyd asked.

The question was surreal. Adam Wales was dead. Murdered. The body had been cremated. There had been thousands of mourners. How could Floyd possibly tell him anything?

"This is a practical joke, isn't it?" I asked.

"No."

"Seriously, Floyd, stop playing. Because I know you are playing. I'm just a well-known ex-hustler you admired in East 94th. And by the way, I do remember the apartment. It was that rich kid's coming out party and he had invited the whole of Manhattan. It was such a big event, you may not even have been there. I was big word of mouth news then. Everyone thought I was his date, or should I say his acquisition? The gay press even printed photos."

"I was there," Floyd added.

"So what was this phone call you had today, and what does it have to do with seeing me here?"

"Accident. Glorious accident, Michael."

He paused, as if suddenly reluctant to go on.

"I am listening," I said.

"Adam rang me this afternoon. He's been sleeping badly. He wanted some company late tonight around twelve, and asked me to discreetly find someone who could be trusted to stay the night with him and be discreet about it. I came here for dinner and then I saw you. It's as simple as that."

"But it's not simple." I almost pounded the table in frustration. "Stop fucking with my mind. Who was it they found if it wasn't Adam Wales thirty years ago?"

I had to be blunt. I had to burst the bubble of the story I was hearing. Let Floyd whatever his name (in my frustration I could not remember it) answer that. He did.

"Adam had a lookalike who came from Arkansas: a strange boy who had no family to speak of. No friends. Adam fell in love with him, but of course back then he was known to be completely straight. No one knew."

"Please, Floyd, no more seventies clichés. What really happened?"

"This lookalike got too much power over Adam. One night Adam took him to his apartment. The concierge was sick or something, so no one saw them go up. The boy was going to spill, and Adam knew it. So he smashed his face and body until it was unrecognisable and staged the death, dressing the body in his own clothes. He said to me afterwards, it was as if he had killed an angel."

"Very pretty," I said sceptically. "Then what happened?"

"The body was found. Adam had made the scene look like a robbery, although the police could find no traces of anyone breaking in. Hollywood hushed up the rumours that the whole thing was suspicious. The police were told to shut their mouths. Case closed. Adam Wales, the greatest new star of a generation was officially dead. His films made a whole new fortune and Adam had plastic surgery done to his face."

"Ridiculous. Sounds like an old Lizabeth Scott movie."

Floyd laughed.

"Oh, you really will get on with Adam," he said. "*Stolen Face* was a film he saw as a child. It made him want to act. He felt the same way about her as you felt about him."

"But I wanted Adam in my bed."

"As a child, Adam wanted Lizabeth Scott in his. He's had women in his life as well as men. Not as serious, but he has had them. I assume you are—"

"—strictly homo."

"Don't tell him that."

"I'm not going to tell him anything, because all this is just a pack of lies—some dark story you have made up to—"

I shut up and looked down at the table. Floyd said nothing and we sat like that in silence for what seemed like a long time. The waiter who had served us began to roam around the table, hoping no doubt that we would at last order something else.

"I think I should get the check," I said at last.

Ignoring this remark, Floyd murmured slowly and clearly, "You're the right person for him to see tonight. He wants someone around your age. He is tired of young people. He wants to talk. And he will like your looks."

I made a sign to the waiter and asked for the check.

"Adam Wales didn't kill anyone," I said. "He was no murderer. I don't believe any of it"

"He preferred retirement from the world to being exposed by that boy as a homosexual."

"Yeah," I said flatly and paid the waiter. "Now I am ready to go."

"Michael, you were a first rate hustler, and you lived for risk. I am asking you a great favour now and I'm asking you to take a risk, one more time."

It was then that I had the intuition that what Floyd was

telling me was true. I'd had this experience before in my life. First you don't believe in something, then quite abruptly and even without understanding why, you accept what is told, and accept it as fact.

"Where did you say he lives?"

"An apartment on 5th. I'll take you there if you decide to come. You see, I am the only person who knows the truth about Adam."

"That you know of," I repeated automatically.

"That I know of. But I like to believe it's true."

"How has he managed it all these years? I mean hiding out in New York on a street like that?"

"The name is different, the face is different."

Nothing more was said between us after that. We left the restaurant together. We caught a cab, and in a short while we were there. Floyd had keys and we went up in the elevator to the apartment. It was the last apartment at the top of the building. He opened the door in silence and I entered after him. The entrance was lit by candlelight and from there I saw a warren of rooms, all lit by candles. I wanted to ask about the candles, but when I tried to speak to Floyd I found he was no longer beside me and that the apartment door was being closed behind me. I was alone. In a moment of panic I tried the door. It was locked. Without a key there was no way out. My first impulse was to cry for help. An inner voice reminded me that the Adam Wales I had been told about was a murderer and that I was possibly on dangerous ground. Then my sense of curiosity overtook my fear and I stepped into the room that was immediately facing me. It was brightly lit by candles and at the far end there was a long window overlooking Central Park. Between the door and the window were a few objects of antique furniture and, to my astonishment, a tall piece of sculpture standing in the centre of the room. It gleamed white in the candlelight and approaching it I saw that it was made entirely from one piece of marble. Two figures stood, one below the other—a young woman in front, and behind her, clasping her half-naked body, the totally naked body of an angel who was leaning forward. Her head leant back close to his. They were caught in the instant before a kiss, and as I drew closer to them, I allowed myself to imagine that they were not marble, but flesh. The kiss would be made and they would make love. The male angel's wings seemed to beat in a permanent silence.

"Beautiful, isn't it?"

I heard his voice. I recognised his voice. It was the voice I had heard so many times on the screen. I was so afraid I could not move. I looked at the statue as if for help. They were, at that moment, more capable of movement than I was. I stared at the male angel's face, at his beauty of line and proportion. The flickering of the candlelight and the sudden rush of air in the room gave the impression that the angel's face was alive and that his lips, half-parted for a kiss, would speak back to me if I went up to him and talked.

"She had dreams of meeting an angel. He, looking down at her from heaven, desired her so much that he took on human form to be near her. She accepted the impossible. She accepted that his wings would have to remain to remind her that he was not entirely of this earth. She had no choice. How could she refuse an angelic lover?"

He made no move towards me, nor did I turn to look at him. I was not ready to look at him. I continued staring at the woman and the angel.

"She has her eyes closed," I said. "Can she see him?"

"She knows he is there. She can feel his body. She can hear the beating of his wings. He is on the point of kissing her lips. But her eyes, yes, her eyes are still closed."

"It must be hard for her to believe that at last she has made her angel real."

"Or that he has succeeded in breaking away from his angelic solitude to come to her. I would say there is disbelief on both sides. But there is certainly desire."

"Oh yes," I said.

58

I heard him as he crossed the room. Light, soft steps on the wooden floors. I felt a hand touch my arm, and then the hard grasp of fingers on my flesh.

"Are you really Adam?" I asked. I still would not turn around.

"Is that important?"

"I just—I mean—I don't want to be told lies. Like your sleeping. Are you having difficulty sleeping at the moment?"

"Yes, that's true. Too many nightmares. Too many memories of a past that is gone, that was, and isn't anymore."

"Floyd told me you killed a man, that you faked your own death."

"It's true."

"Because you were afraid people would know about your sexuality?"

"Yes."

The voice was soft. Soft as the steps had been. I was dreaming again. Once more in that final scene of the film. The last film he had made before his death. The final fadeout was on a kiss. And here I was, waiting for it.

"I'm in my late-fifties," I said. "I am no longer young, and I have scars on my chest and back. I gave up hustling after an attack in a park, back in the eighties."

He laughed. The quietest of laughs. I had seen him laugh once on screen, just before a young man provoked him to a fight. He had been wearing a red jacket and had looked very, very beautiful.

"Floyd promised me the best in town," he said softly. "You have a solid back. I like that."

I made a move to turn then, but he pressed my arm tightly and said, "No, no, remain as you are for a while longer. I can sense that you will not disappoint me, but I may disappoint you. Floyd told you they gave me a different face?"

"Yes."

"It was a botched job, but good enough. I didn't exactly have time to get the best surgeon in town, or even the next best. Not everyone can be bought."

"Not even me." I whispered this and he withdrew his hand.

"Does that mean—?"

I interrupted him and said, "It only means that if I stay, I stay for free. Let me put it another way. If you are Adam Wales, then I have come for you and not for your money."

I turned round then and closing my eyes I took him in my arms. His body was compact and smaller than mine. He had appeared tall on the screen, but then so many beautiful men did. He buried his face on my shoulder. I opened my eyes, and in the candlelight I saw that his hair was almost as white as the marble of the statue. I kissed his hair with my lips. Then he raised his face, and in the gentle light I saw a lined face, carved cruelly by both man and age. And yet, the eyes—the eyes glowed and flickered as they had glowed and flickered on the screen. I was staring into an immense close-up of his eyes, and I remembered them from all the times I had seen them before. It was miraculously true. He was Adam Wales.

"Adam," I said.

"I don't know your name," he replied.

"Michael."

"Maybe I met you—I mean before—"

I stopped what he was going to say by pressing his lips upon my lips. We stood there in front of the statue, clasping each other and kissing. It was all I wanted to do. That night it was all he wanted to do. The rest of it we spent talking. I learned about his boyhood, youth and later years. I even listened to him describe killing the boy he had loved. Just before dawn he fell asleep in my arms, and I began to see the things in his apartment by the light of day, and with the light, none of the magic of this meeting went away.

I remember it was eleven o'clock in the morning when we made love. I heard a clock strike in his hallway. At that moment I became Adam Wales's lover, and I still am.

SNOW

The white night of his sleep had been shot with darkness: voices heard, faces fleetingly seen, rising to the surface then plunging back into the dark, then suddenly the awakening and the too harsh light. His eyes had struggled to accept the solidity of form after the liquid shapes that had been his world. He could move his body now, look around him, see objects, touch them, and move—the amazing realisation of movement, however unsteady at first. Then he was brought home to rest and adjust.

"My name is Robert," he said, standing naked in front of a full length mirror. He reached out to touch the mirror. It did not dissolve as it would have done in the endless (had it really come to an end?) and ever-changing landscape of his dreams.

"My name is Robert and I am solid again. This is where I live. I live in Brighton."

He stared at his body in the mirror. In that long sleep he had touched his body so often, but this time he could see himself doing it. The exact motion of his hand as it touched his stomach and then his neck was lucidly reflected back at him. In the dream the touching was never so exact. If he dreamt he was caressing his genitals, it would change to him touching his hair. He would touch his open eyes and his fingers would enter the fluid quite easily, without disturbance, without pain. He put his hand to his face and watched in the mirror as his fingers approached his eyes. He pointed a finger at his right eye, then homed in on it, paused and withdrew. Unlike in that long, long sleep, he knew the finger plunging into his eye would cause harm and pain. He stepped forward and looked at his body more closely. It had changed. The flesh was not as tight as distant memory told him it should be.

His chest was covered with more hair than before and the lines on his face were deeper, more accentuated. He stared at his eyes and saw that they had an expression of sorrow in them. His brown eyes looked mournful and full of loss. You have lost so much time to another reality, they said. His eyes spoke to him more clearly than any spoken word, yet he had to say it aloud to himself.

"I have lost so much time. I cannot bring it back."

His mouth was more thin-lipped: two thin lines opening and shutting, and in between, yellowish teeth.

"I used to have white teeth."

He said the words loudly, enunciating clearly, opening his mouth wider as he did so. His teeth had changed, and yet they were all there. He turned away from his reflection. He looked away from the mirror and stared at the room around him. It was book-lined as it had always been, and memory made him cross the room to a large dictionary. He took it out and there, in between the page that separated S from T, he found a letter. The letter had been opened, yet he could not bring himself to take it out. He had hidden the letter there, many years ago. He shut the dictionary and replaced it on the shelf.

"Not now," he said. "Not yet. Not until—"

He paused on the word until. Until when? Until another endless stretch of time had passed?

"I am fifty-five years old, and the coma, my long sleep started years ago. They told me how long, but I don't remember."

He closed his eyes to prevent his tears from falling, but a wet trickle filtered its way through, moistening his cheeks. He rubbed the tears away. Then there was a knock on the door and automatically he called out, "Come in." An elderly man stepped into the room and smiled at him. The smile was wary, and when the voice spoke it sounded cautious.

"I'm sorry. You are not dressed."

The unknown man reached for a dressing gown hanging behind the door and handed it to him. There was a familiarity in this gesture that he faintly remembered.

"I brought you here from the hospital. You don't remember me, do you? You seemed to remember me then. The private nurse I got for you told me you are fully aware, fully rested and that with my care I can take you out. But you are still not sure about me, are you?"

He felt flustered with mounting panic. He wanted to remember this man. He looked at the lines on the man's face. He was probably the same age as himself, but then again they were perhaps of a man in his sixties. He vaguely recalled a man much younger.

"Robert, I'm Alan. I am your best friend."

"Oh," he replied, and tightened the belt on his dressing gown.

"It will take time," Alan said.

"Alan—?"

He had a memory of being held as he sobbed in this man's arms. The arms had been firm and strong. They had been standing beside his lover's bed. His lover had just died.

"Simpson," Alan replied. "Alan Simpson."

"Yes."

The smile on Alan's face grew larger, gratified that recall was coming back so quickly. Robert watched as Alan brushed against him, going to the bed in his study and making the bed for him.

"Did you sleep well? You were very tired when we brought you back. I was with Tim. But you wouldn't know Tim. I met him after—"

He watched as Alan straightened out the creases on the bedspread. He watched this man who was his oldest friend pick up cushions from off the floor and spread them over the perfectly made bed.

"You always liked perfection," he said automatically, realising he had seized on a perception of this man that he had always known, but had for such a long emptiness of time forgotten.

"Yes, my one failing," Alan replied rather camply. "I was always the one to pick and choose. And at last I did. I chose Tim. A little late, but better late than never as the cliché goes."

"Is he nice, this Tim?"

"*Very* nice."

The accent on the very was deep and low and underlined. Robert sat on the bed, momentarily hesitant about ruffling its flat landscape. Alan sat down on a chair beside one of the tall bookshelves. He took out a packet of cigarettes and waved it.

"Do you mind?" he asked. "We have to ask now. It's not the done thing anymore to smoke without asking. We have to accentuate the health risk."

Robert laughed. He laughed at what Alan had just said, and it was as if an invisible ice had been broken. So much had changed and he wanted to know it all.

"Tell me," he said.

"Tell you what?"

"About it?"

"About what?"

"All of what has happened. So much must have happened during—" again he paused, seeking the euphemism, "—that long sleep."

"Yes, but not now. You must get dressed and not be shy about me. We were lovers once and I have seen your body."

"It's changed, hasn't it? That too has changed."

Alan smiled and drew on his cigarette. He then sighed and looked down at the carpet.

"I'm in my sixties. I was younger when we last talked. Think of it. I looked as if perhaps youth was still a part of me then. And now? How time has caught up with me. But don't worry, you're still handsome. You'll do fine."

Finishing his cigarette, Alan stood up and went to the wardrobe.

"Now, let me choose you something that is passable for the twenty-first century. You must have something classical here."

Alan opened the wardrobe and Robert watched as Alan picked out a grey suit and a white shirt. He laughed at the choice and his eye lingered over a leather jacket that he suddenly remembered.

"Why not that?" he said, pointing.

"No dear, no. It's so, well, day before yesterday. The cut is all wrong. For your first time facing the world, put on this lovely neutral suit. I see you have a grey tie to match and grey shoes. After all, you were in banking."

He hadn't given a thought to work, or what his social position had been. He saw himself calculating, calculating, and piles of money growing endlessly, then coming crashing down.

"It all crashed," he said suddenly. "They told me that. It was one of the first things they told me."

"What Robert? What went crash?"

"In the hospital. They told me. Everything crashed."

He looked at Alan as if expecting him to elaborate on this mass destruction of the world he had lived in. Instead, Alan reassured him that they were just in a recession, but in safe hands as there was now a Conservative government, albeit propped up by others. Alan added that this was an unfortunate compromise, but necessary. Robert made no reply to all this information and reached out to take the suit and shirt from Alan.

"Thank you for telling me," he said simply, then went and reached for some underwear at the bottom of the wardrobe. "It's all so ridiculous," he added.

Alan raised his eyebrows at this flippant response in mock surprise. Chain-smoking, he lit another cigarette.

"Do you want me to give you a list of other major events?"

"It's alright. I'll find out in time."

He dressed slowly, awkwardly. His fingers refused to tie his tie and Alan stepped in to help. After the job was done he put his arms round his best friend and hugged him close.

"I do want to remember you so much," he said, closing his

eyes. He then felt Alan pushing him away gently.

"Tim is in a taxi. He's been waiting all this time, expensively and patiently, to take us out for dinner. He must be freezing cold, poor darling, but then you perhaps haven't realised England is frozen at the moment. Snow everywhere. Just like in a fairy-tale."

"Snow?" he questioned, his eyes opening wide. The word snow made him suddenly afraid. "I don't like snow," he whispered, more to himself than to Alan. "I don't like the white of snow. It was like that for so long for me. An endless white. I cannot describe it."

"And neither should you," replied Alan dismissively. "No more morbid thoughts about all that. All you need to remember is some idiot crashed your car. He died, and you— well, princess, you went into a long sleep. We never thought—"

Alan stopped.

"That I would wake up again?" Robert asked.

"I said no more morbid thoughts. Tim will have turned into a snowman in that freezing taxi, and for once I am not going to spend hours blowing on him to warm him up."

Outside in the street he was dazzled by the white. The pavements were covered with snow, but the road itself had been cleared. A few flakes fell on him as he was propelled towards a waiting car.

"Now don't you worry," Alan said, "Tim knows exactly where we are going."

A young man stepped out of the taxi and opened the door for him. He let himself be bundled into the back seat. Alan sat in front and the young man sat beside him.

"I'm going to introduce him all over again," Alan said, turning and tapping Tim on the shoulder.

"Tim, Robert. Robert, Tim."

"Pleased to meet you, Tim."

He felt his hand being firmly grasped. It was a pleasant

sensation to be touched again by a good-looking man, and in the dim light he could see that Tim was exceptionally good-looking. He had blond hair, blue eyes and a smile that sparkled. No yellow teeth for him, Robert thought.

"Isn't he lovely," Alan said laughing, "and far too young. In hotels they think we are father and son. He's all of twenty-six."

"It isn't important," Tim mumbled. "What is important is this fucking weather. The worst in God knows how long, or so they say. And it's Brighton. Why should it fucking snow in Brighton?"

Robert winced, hoping the taxi-man would not be offended by this language. He tried to remember when he had last seen the reality of snow, and not the white floating that had resembled it in his dreams. He tried hard to remember, but failed.

Tim turned to him in the back of the taxi and asked, "How are you feeling?" Robert noticed that he had a slight Scottish accent. It was a sexy voice and he was surprised to feel that he was getting an erection.

"As Alan must have so delicately put it to you, I'm not totally out of it yet," he replied, "but thanks for asking."

"We are taking you to a quiet restaurant," Tim added. "The food is good too."

Alan interrupted by saying that the food was also lightly cooked, and good for the digestion. He wanted to be careful about Robert's digestion.

"He's like a nurse to me," Robert said.

He was directing his statement to Tim, who laughed and turned to look at him. Robert caught his eye and smiled. He was glad of this moment of complicity. It felt like flirting. He was awake, and he was sitting in the back of a taxi with a handsome young man. Then the dark thought hit his mind that he had been in a car with another handsome young man when the car had crashed and he had entered his so-called sleep. He looked out of the taxi window. All he could see was extreme white against extreme dark.

"Why did I ever come to this city?" he asked aloud. "It is a city now, isn't it? I think I heard that in the hospital."

"To your second question, yes it is. To the first, because we all love you here," Alan said. "And it's close to far too expensive London. You made your money there, and you found your lovely home, much cheaper, here."

He looked out of the window again and saw that they were travelling along Brighton seafront and everything was so dreadfully dark on white. In a moment he thought absurdly, we will all be plunged into the darkness of the sea.

"How far is it from here?" he asked nervously.

"We thought we'd have a drink first," Alan replied. "A new bar, recently opened. It's better than the others."

He leant back in the taxi and without realising it, rested his head on Tim's shoulder and fell into a light sleep. He felt peaceful, mercifully peaceful, but then out of the semi-sleep he was jolted awake by the sudden vision of a screaming face. He was looking down on the face of his lover who was dying and screaming at the same time. The word AIDS branded itself on his brain.

"Oh, my God," he cried aloud.

"What is it?" Alan asked, his voice was clear and sounded frightened.

Robert opened his eyes, withdrew his head from Tim's shoulder and stared again at the white of the snow on the pavements outside the moving car. Bright lights from the street lamps above sent glittering reflections back at him. The car stopped. He heard Tim's voice.

"We can go back if you are feeling ill."

"No, no, I'm not," he said. Sweat was breaking out on his forehead. He wanted to forget the image he had seen of his lover, and then in the next second he knew he would never forget and that he never should. It was his lasting legacy, dead or alive. Ian. That had been his lover's name. He remembered clearly now.

"I thought of Ian," he said, and Alan turned to face him.

"Are you sure you are well enough?"

It was Tim again, Tim who had spoken. And in the question, he sensed a hope in the voice that he was well enough. He realised with a sense of obscure pain that Tim in some way wanted him to be there.

"Tim is worried about you," Alan added. "So am I. You might not be ready for this."

"I think we should have our drink and then have our dinner as arranged," Robert said to them both. He felt strong now and wanted to show that he could be assertive.

"I'm ready," Tim said.

The bar was full of older men. He saw that when he entered the room. It was all shiny and shimmering, and overdone with Christmas decorations. The place was also dotted with long mauve coloured sofas.

"Not as I remember things," he muttered.

He was led to one of the sofas by Tim who seemed to help him down onto it as if he were very old indeed. From desire for Tim he now looked at him with a sort of intuitive dislike. He felt as if this young man was patronising him in some way, desiring him too perhaps, but hating it.

"I'll get the drinks," Tim said. "What do you two want?"

"Vodka, please. Straight," Alan replied and sat down next to Robert.

"Just a beer," Robert heard himself say, and with a look close to disappointment, Tim moved away.

"I get the feeling he wanted me to order something more in keeping with this place," he said, looking at Alan who smiled and said nothing. "I suppose it is a rather common choice for a bar like this," he added.

"Tim is young," Alan replied, as if this explained everything.

"Yes, I see."

There was a moment's uncomfortable pause, then he

looked away from Alan and at the men around them.

"Do they like this loungey atmosphere?" he asked.

"It was beginning when we last went out together," Alan replied defensively.

"You mean it has now taken hold?"

"I suppose so."

Tim returned with the drinks. Robert noticed Tim was drinking something purple. He had no idea what it was, nor for that matter did he care to ask.

"You must feel a bit out of place with so many older men around you?" Robert said. He smiled at Tim who sat down beside him. He suddenly felt uncomfortable being in the middle of Alan and Tim and longed for an old-fashioned room with conventional tables and separate chairs.

"He likes older men," Alan replied crisply for him.

Tim smiled in return and drank his purple drink.

Robert knew then what he had to ask, and putting down his beer because his hands were starting to shake, he dared to pose the question. He knew before he asked what the reply would be, but he had to ask. For Ian's sake he had to ask.

"What's the date today?"

Tim looked at Alan in a puzzled way. He looked as if he hadn't a clue.

"December 1st," Alan said.

"Yes. And?" Tim asked.

"World AIDS Day." Robert replied coldly.

Tim coughed. The sort of cough that could be real, meant as a signal for let's get out of here, or a nervous reply in itself.

"Yes," Alan said and drank his vodka. Having finished his drink he asked Tim to get him another one. Out of earshot of Tim, Alan turned to Robert and said quietly, "He doesn't like to talk about AIDS, nor do his friends. They don't relate much to World AIDS Day. Of course they know about the annual vigil. Tim does too, but he wants to forget it." He paused, then added, "The way you said it, it was all in capital letters. It's not like that anymore."

"How is it like?" he asked.

"Unspoken for some," Alan said.

"Unspoken? But why? The whole city should be at the vigil, snow or no fucking snow." There was a desperation in his voice that seemed to be torn out of his throat. Tim must have heard it as he returned with the vodka and repeat drinks for both himself and Robert.

"Don't let's say any more," Alan murmured.

"I heard that," Tim said. "Say what?"

"About AIDS." Robert very nearly shouted the words. He felt like he had a fever and a feeling of panic made him fear that he could lose his self-control. He finished his beer and quickly downed the second. Tim shifted awkwardly on the sofa. Robert turned and stared at the young man. As he moved the lower part of his body he felt his aching erection return.

"I was asking Alan why some people of your age don't remember this day." He paused. "Don't you know it's important to remember?"

Alan interrupted with a flurried "please" that sounded at the same time frightened and cold as ice. He gripped Robert on the arm tightly, signalling for him to stop.

"It's a simple question," Robert continued, staring at Tim. He wanted to bruise the young man's mouth with a kiss and at the same time to bruise him elsewhere into some kind of awareness.

"Why are you ignoring this day?" he persisted.

"What bloody day?" Now Tim had had enough. "I don't know what the hell you are talking about."

"Today, Tim, today. In memory of those who have died. In solidarity with those who are suffering."

"I'm not suffering." Tim was angry. Robert had made him angry. "I'm taking my meds. So are my friends. It's all under control. I'm under control."

"I can see it," Robert said sarcastically.

"Don't be so fucking clever." Tim looked at him with fierce anger as he said this.

"I think I've had enough," Alan added quietly with a sort of defeat.

Robert watched as they both got up to go and he stood up as well. He wanted to ask questions. He wanted to ask about the medications Tim took. There was so much he wanted to know and yet, in this mauve paradise, he knew he would be unable to get any answers. He would have to wait.

"The evening is ruined," he said and looked at Alan. "I know I should apologise, but somehow I can't. It's just all a horrible question. One day soon, I hope, I will get the right answer."

Ignoring what he had to say, Alan moved to the door. Tim looked at Robert and for a moment there was a gentleness in his voice as he asked, "At least let me find you a taxi home."

"No thank you," he replied. He looked at Tim and saw the face of a world he had missed, and that he would have to come to know. "Take care," he said to Tim, and sat down. He watched as they both left him alone in the bar. Unsteady on his feet he ordered another beer, and leaning back on the sofa he made a mental image of the letter he would open when he got back home. It was a simple letter. He read it in his mind, although to feel the full healing power of it he would have to hold it in his hand.

Be brave my love and face the future whatever comes. Remember that I will love you always.
Ian

ACCIDENTAL MEETING

Witek felt suddenly breathless as he left the train. He admitted to himself that he was tired and trying hard to suppress his guilt. It had also been a particularly tedious journey. He had not done it in ten years. He had been in his early twenties back then, but still found the long haul through Germany tiring, and the slow trawl through the Netherlands, too long. From the Dutch border onwards he had been in a carriage with a screaming child, and as the train was full he had been unable to change seats. He blamed the noise for giving him the ache in his head, but now released from that disturbance found he not only still felt the pain but was also experiencing difficulty breathing. He sat on the terrace of the *Grand-café Eerste Klas* on Amsterdam Centraal Station and ordered a black coffee with a glass of water. When the waiter returned with his order he took two paracetamol.

I have come back, he thought. I must calm myself. I must try to forget those terrible images I left behind me.

He drank the coffee and looked around him. The interior of the station seemed to be as it had always been, a little cleaner perhaps, but then everything was a little cleaner than it had been ten years ago. Yet at the same time, the people passing appeared scruffier. He smiled as he recalled how he had always considered the Dutch badly dressed. A Polish woman could make herself elegant with next to nothing, yet with all their disposable income, Dutch women were unimaginative in their choice of clothes. He smiled too as he saw quite a number of them wearing brown furry boots that appeared ridiculously heavy. He sipped his coffee and observed, and at the back of his mind was the thought, Ewa does not dress like this. She is always so surprising in the choices she makes and looks more refined than these women ever will. Then he contradicted himself and told himself he was being unfair about the people around him, and that anyway, quite a lot of them were probably tourists and not Dutch at all. But still the prejudice remained that the women he saw had none of the innate elegance of Polish women. He finished his coffee and felt alien and alone. Why had he come back to this country? Why had he chosen Amsterdam and not Berlin? Berlin was so much larger. Couldn't he have escaped better in the crowds there? And yet, outside of the familiarity of Warsaw, Amsterdam was what he knew best. He saw Ewa's face, twisted away from him as she lay on the floor. He wanted to hit the image out of his head with his hands. He wanted to beat himself into forgetfulness. And then at that moment he knew that he must drink. He called the waiter over and asked for a large beer.

"Drinking again," he whispered to himself. "This is how it begins, as it began in those bars over ten years ago. I wanted to forget then, but then there were other reasons why. I always drink when I am on the run from life."

An older man at a neighbouring table was looking at him. He was sitting alongside the man, at a distance, but he had noticed the persistent stare. He turned slightly to look at the man, who smiled back at him.

I'm no longer for sale, he thought, immediately assuming, perhaps wrongly, that this was the man's intention. When the waiter came with the beer he drank it down too fast. Far too fast. He gasped for breath, and feeling giddy, reached to touch his suitcase. He needed something to ease the giddiness and opening the suitcase, took out a book of Polish poetry. He placed it on the table in front of him, then gestured to the waiter again. He ordered another beer. A few minutes later, the older man was standing by his table, staring down at him.

"Do you speak English?" the man asked.

Witek looked up at him. The man had a lined, but not unpleasant face. He was still smiling. Witek did not return the smile.

"Yes," he replied abruptly.

"I believe I know your face. It was a long time ago, and you have changed, but I am sure I have seen you before."

Witek shrugged. He did not want to make contact with anyone so soon. He would not look at the man and instead of looking at him, stared again at the people passing. He was also tired and feeling unwell, and this man was a tiresome intrusion. Whatever the man wants, he thought, I do not.

"Aren't you Polish?"

The bars. Of course. He could avoid the inevitable no longer. The man had recognised him, although, as he had said, he had changed. He looked up at the man and said neutrally, "Won't you sit down?"

The man, still smiling, sat down next to him.

"I'll join you in a beer, if I may," the man said, adding, "Would you like another?"

Witek laughed. He recognises me for the drunk I was and which in times of crisis I will always be. Already the beer was making him feel lighter. He felt the slow anaesthetic cover his inner pain, his hidden, disturbing images. Slowly the prostrate figure of Ewa lying on the floor was receding. He wanted to believe that he no longer cared about what had happened and, oh yes, the drink would help. The drink would help it all to fade from view.

"Yes, thank you. I will have another." And another, he added to himself. Let them pile up like a barrier to hide me.

"Your name is?"

"Witek."

At that moment the waiter, far too blond and far too pretty, came back to the table. The beers were ordered. Witek looked at the young man's back as he walked away. He felt a sudden desire to throw the young man violently face downwards onto a bed. He imagined pulling down the man's trousers and penetrating him.

"I am Alec."

The sexual image broke up in Witek's mind as he raised a new glass of beer to his lips. He reluctantly looked at the man, but said nothing in return. After a few moments silence Alec added, "An Englishman who has been here too long and seen too many people."

"And you believe that includes me?" Witek replied sarcastically.

"I may be mistaken."

English politeness. God, how they bore me—always sounding as if they are reading from a book. No music in the voice. No melody. Just that endless droning. But instead of saying that he replied quickly and simply, "I was here many years ago. Ten years ago. Were you here ten years ago?"

Alec said he was.

"Then it is quite possible we may have seen each other. Amsterdam is a small city."

"Indeed it is."

Witek looked down at the table. Looked at his book. Alec, noticing this, looked at the book as well. Then automatically, Witek opened it.

"Poetry," Alec said.

"You recognise the name? Zbigniew Herbert. My favourite poet. He soothes me. The long journey from Warsaw unsettled me. I was going to read for a while."

"When I disturbed you," Alec added.

Witek looked at him, and he suddenly felt very serious.

"Do you really believe you know me?" he asked.

"I don't say that I have known you, but I am sure that I have seen you. There is a difference, isn't there?"

The nervous smile. The understatement. Witek knew quite well what he meant.

"I do not remember you," he said.

"Ah, but you would not have been looking."

The conversation became extremely fluid from then on, quite literally, as the beers came quickly and were drunk fast. What they said to each other for the next hour or so Witek was unable to remember later. He drank and he drank, and when they both got up from the table he was conscious only that Alec had paid the bill. He noticed nothing when they left the station and passively allowed himself to be led. He even let Alec carry his suitcase. Then the apartment. Then a sudden explosion of darkness as he passed out.

He woke up in a single bed. He had no idea what time it was. There was no clock by the bed, and all his belongings, including his watch, were gone. He was naked and alone.

"Hello," he called out loudly.

The sound of feet coming. Alec was standing by his bed; his lined face smiling down at him. Witek was wide awake now, and felt a moment of panic. I must have been undressed by him, but I cannot recall any of it.

"I must go," he said. He could not get out of the bed, not until Alec had left the room, and he could not ask him to leave a room in his own apartment. He was alarmingly conscious and lucid, and at the same time hated the confusions of his situation.

"You must have taken my clothes off," he said.

"You drank too much and were unable to do it yourself," Alec replied simply. "You passed out. I put you to bed in the spare room."

"But why are my clothes not here? Not even my watch. I must know if—"

"No," Alec interrupted him. "Nothing happened."

"You undressed me. You looked at me. You did want to look at me, didn't you?"

He said the words flatly, and as he said them he realised he didn't care. Let the man have his thrill.

Alec looked down at him and said nothing. He neither admitted nor denied.

"How long have I been asleep?"

"It was dark when we got back. You slept all night—a good twelve hours."

There was a moment's uneasy pause.

"Is there an hotel we should notify?" Alec asked in that ultra-polite way Witek disliked so much.

"No, there's no hotel," he replied, irritated.

"Then there is no hurry. You must eat something before you go."

Witek shrugged passively. Every time he was with an older man he felt passive: a state that was quite contrary to his normal behaviour. Passive, as he had been ten years ago. He stared up at Alec, and for a moment he had forgotten Alec's name. He just wanted to get out of the straitjacket of the bed and be active.

"I would like a drink first. Before breakfast," he said with a note of aggression in his voice. "I guess it's obvious I drink too much," he laughed. "Also, I have forgotten your name."

"Alec," Alec said and left the room.

"My clothes. I need my clothes," he called after him.

He dressed quickly once his clothes were brought, and then in Alec's living room asked for the drink. Alec offered him beer. He drank two. Then he needed the bathroom and, once inside, voided his bowels realising he had not done so in 48 hours. He showered and returned to find a large breakfast waiting.

"English style," Alec said with a trace of mockery in his voice.

Witek looked at the plate of warm eggs and greasy bacon. He had not eaten in a long while except for a rotten train sandwich that he had thrown aside after one mouthful. He ate the breakfast rapidly but avoided the tea, which he had always hated.

"I was hungry."

He pushed the plate away, and asked for more beer. Tension was building in the back of his neck. Already, Ewa was returning to his mind, and he wanted desperately to ignore the memory of what had happened.

"I really need alcohol," he said.

Alec was kind enough to say nothing, and Witek had one

beer, and then another. He realised he was still in shock.

He had been in shock on Warsaw station while he waited five hours for a train. Strikes in Germany or something. He had paced the large concourse of the station, glancing outside occasionally as if expecting to be followed and then seized. He had felt empty and sick inside. All he had for comfort were Zbigniew Herbert's poems which he had grabbed from a bookshelf before fleeing the house. He had promised himself to read every word of the book on the way to Amsterdam, but in the end he hadn't even opened it.

"Have I aged much?" he asked while Alec was getting him another beer. "Please tell me."

"Older," Alec replied, stating the obvious. "It's good to be older."

Witek smiled.

"Is it? Why is it?"

"I am speaking for myself, I suppose," Alec added. "Getting older for me means I am coming nearer to the end."

"How old are you?"

"In my fifties. I was in my forties when—"

Alec looked at Witek and smiled.

"When you saw me?" Witek asked.

"Yes. You would sit at the bar night after night, drinking a lot and hardly ever talking to anyone. I never saw you talk to the other Poles there. I tried to approach you, but you seemed to have an invisible shield around you. I couldn't work out any way to get you to see me, to look at me, or smile. I think once I saw you with a man."

Witek went to where Alec kept his beers, and took one for himself.

"If you had stayed in the bar 'til closing, you would have seen me leave last. It's true, I hardly ever went with anyone. I was hopeless at the job."

He looked at Alec while he raised the bottle directly to his mouth.

"If I had met you then, you would have been a job, that's

all. And I didn't like the work."

Alec suddenly became very busy clearing the table. Witek watched for a while in silence and knew somehow that these last words had offended him; that perhaps he had destroyed some long held illusion—but it was the truth. He remembered how so many of the men had mistakenly gone to those bars looking for love.

"I'm married," he said suddenly.

He had to say it. Ewa, and the image of Ewa and how he had left her, was there, darkly in his mind. He saw the red blood stains on her dress. This was the last image of her that he had. The last image recorded in his mind as he closed the door and hurried to the station.

"Where is she?" Alec asked.

"I hurt her. I hurt her badly."

Witek returned to the table, sat down and put his head in his hands. Alec came and sat next to him. Witek felt the touch of his hand on his arm.

"Do you want to talk about it?"

Then, as if finally doing what he had wanted to do for days, Witek began to cry. The tears wet his fingers. He was ashamed of letting go like this in front of a man he barely knew. He could not remember ever having cried in front of a man before.

"I beat her up," he said slowly. "I beat her up. Her body. Her face. With my hands." He took his hands away from his face and stared at them. "It was not the first time, but it was the hardest. Then I left her. She was lying on the floor and there was blood on her clothes. I made her bleed." He paused. "With my hands. With these hands I made her bleed."

Alec brought him another drink and he drank it down in one go. Now he wanted to tell the whole story, and the words seemed to pour out of him.

"I married her after I left Amsterdam. I had known her since we were children. We went out together as teenagers, and she knew I was restless to see other countries, to find myself as I liked to tell her. That is why I read Zbigniew Herbert. He travelled so much, when it was difficult for a Pole to travel. He had little money like me, but he travelled a lot. He made it his priority." He paused. "I don't write. I can't write, but I have always loved to read. Especially poetry." He stopped and stared around the room. "You don't have any books," he said.

"I don't read much," Alec replied. "It's never been my thing. In England I worked as an engineer. Then I had an accident with my leg. That's why I limp, or maybe you hadn't noticed. Anyway, I got compensation. I have enough to live on. I like it here."

"Are you alone?" Witek asked.

"Let's say I have long distance friends. But tell me about your wife."

Witek got up and began to pace the room. He was crying again, and in walking he hoped to hide his tears.

"It was a mistake. I did not love her. But she loved me. When I returned to Poland ten years ago, I was emotionally upset and confused, and in my confusion I asked her to marry me. We went and lived in Kraków for a while, but I couldn't stay away from Warsaw, and it was there that I began to do escort work again, without her knowing. I did it because we were so wretchedly poor. I would stay away for days, and after a couple of years she made the decision we should both move back to Warsaw."

He stopped, and for a moment he gasped for air.

"The day I left Warsaw to come back here, I had been with a man. I was stupid and took him back to our place. He had no place, and I was feeling reckless. Maybe I even wanted to put myself into danger. Anyway, she found us naked on our bed. She threw things at the man. She spat at him and cursed him. And when he was gone and I was dressed, she calmed down. But now it was my turn to be furious. I told her I enjoyed it with these men, which wasn't true, and she said I was possessed, that I was a devil. I hit her and couldn't stop hitting her. I told her I had never loved her. I told her I had never wanted her body, and that I had done everything to avoid giving us a child."

"Is that true?" Alec asked.

"It's all true. Except that I didn't tell her *the* truth. The worst part of the truth for her."

"Which is?"

"That I desire young men. That I was in love with a young man in Amsterdam ten years ago, but that I didn't do anything about it at the time. I went out with him. I even went back to his place, where he would beg me to make love to him. I told him that it was wrong to have feelings of desire for another man. That I was a Catholic, and that I would do anything not to be homosexual." He paused and breathed in slowly. "He was German. His name was Volker. He was a student here and I met him when he came to the bar where I was working. He came up to me and we began talking. He didn't know that the men there, including myself, were for sale. When I told him I was like the others, he laughed and said he would change all that. I desired him, but even when he eventually knew that I desired him, I never gave into it. Not even when he offered me money in an act of desperation. It was crazy. I was crazy. I had to leave the city, and him."

Exhausted with talking, Witek sat down. Alec made him coffee. Witek drank it mechanically, and looking at Alec, told him he was grateful, that he thought of him as being very kind.

"I understand Volker," Alec said quietly, and sat next to him. "I think I was a little in love with you myself." He laughed and there was sadness in the laughter. "I don't know what kind of accident made the gods get us together again yesterday. I don't even go to the station often. I was only there to get an English magazine."

Witek took Alec's hand and pressed it hard.

"No one else must love me. No one. Do you understand? Ewa is right. I am possessed. I am a devil."

"Now you are talking like a superstitious Polish idiot. You know that isn't true. Do you know why you got on that train to come back here?"

"I was running."

"Yes, to free yourself. To free yourself to find a young man you can at last respond to. Oh, I know there is the guilt at hitting her and it was a terrible thing to do, but deep down I'm sure you will discover that it was a desire to live that brought you here again. That this place, for all its many faults, is the place where you can hope to find yourself. Or better still, someone else. You know this city, and you know there is more freedom here for gay men than in Poland."

"But Ewa?"

Alec looked at him, and said gently, "Go to the phone. You must have a number you can ring. Ask about her. Just hope you didn't cause her too much harm."

"I can't."

"It's a first step. The hardest you can take."

"I may have killed her."

"You need to know to what extent you harmed her."

"I am afraid, Alec."

"The phone. Now."

With a great deal of hesitation, Witek got up and crossed the room to Alec's phone. He dialled. Ewa's mother picked up the phone. Ewa had several cuts to her face and was emotionally traumatised. She never wanted to see him again. Her mother said that if he returned to Warsaw she would kill him herself, that he was a filthy homosexual and that in God's judgement, and her own, he deserved to die. Witek replied that he would not return and that he was willing to divorce. When he put the phone down his hands began to shake. Then he pitched forward and literally fell into Alec's arms. Alec let him collapse and stroked his hair.

"You will recover from this," he said. "It is not over, this idea of a demon that you have inside of you. It will take patience and a long time to exorcise it."

Witek stayed with Alec for a few more days. He slept, ate a little and drank a lot. He talked about himself constantly, and in his still youthful immaturity did not question Alec about his life. It was only his problems and how he could face life once more, as a man in his early thirties in Amsterdam.

"At least I can work here legally now," he said on the fourth day. They had gone out walking, and he saw an advertisement for a barman in a club on Rembrandtplein.

"Shall I go for it?" he asked Alec.

Alec looked at him with resigned tenderness. It was as if he had brought in a wounded bird out of the cold, and that now the bird was cured, he must give it permission to fly away.

"Of course, you must go for it. And other jobs too."

"Except my old work," Witek said. "Even in Warsaw it was only ever the most desperate men who went with me."

"You are still handsome," Alec observed.

Witek took Alec by the arm, leading him away from Rembrandtplein. Soon they were walking along the Keizersgracht. When they reached a certain house, Witek rang a doorbell.

"It was here," he said nervously. "Volker lived here. Maybe he is still living here."

But Volker had left years before. A youngish man told him he had gone back to Germany. He had met a man and had gone to live with him. Witek smiled and thanked the man. They then returned to Alec's apartment. In silence he went to the single room where he had been sleeping and began to pack his clothes into his suitcase.

"I see you are ready," Alec said slowly.

"I must."

"I know."

Alec smiled at him and Witek felt a surge of tenderness when he saw the barely concealed look of pain on the now familiar lined face.

"You have been good. I will never forget how much easier

you have made it for me. For me to begin to come to terms with myself, and the sort of relationship with another man that I need."

He picked up the book of Zbigniew Herbert that was by his bed and opened it at a page that had a marker in it.

"In the end one cannot keep this love concealed."

He paused after he had translated the words from Polish into English.

"This poem is about so much, so much else, but I've always loved this first line. It goes with me everywhere. And now, perhaps now, I am ready to bring myself out into the light."

He laughed as he closed the book, putting it into his suitcase.

"Do you know, Alec, since I've been here I haven't even noticed that it is spring in the streets. It seemed like winter in Warsaw, yet I did not see the spring there. It had begun and I did not notice it. Only today, after leaving the house where Volker lived, did I notice the first buds on the trees. Wish me luck before I go and please, please let us remain friends."

Alec assured him that he would be there any time he was needed.

THE HOMOSEXUAL
SURREALIST

André Breton expelled homosexuals from the Surrealist movement. He expelled the homosexual dream. This is of perhaps no interest to anyone other than writers and readers who are concerned with the history of Surrealism, or who have an interest or educational need to know about the categorisation of 20th century art movements. It is in many ways a footnote in cultural history that took place nearly one hundred years ago, and is objectively too small to take too seriously against the backdrop of the terrible years preceding that expulsion: the atrocity that was the First World War.

I only began to think about it after I had read René Crevel's work, and then later read accounts of his expulsion from the Surrealist movement. He eventually committed suicide, arguably out of despair at what had happened to him, but also because it was to his mind the only possible act of true freedom in the face of terminal illness. All the details of his young life are there to read for those who want to go further in understanding this man. I personally think he died to efface forever the feelings of betrayal he felt, caused both by his body and by those whom he respected and admired.

I read a couple of his books: *Difficult Death* and then *Babylon*. I also read works by other Surrealists, including *Nadja* by Breton himself. This was a couple of years ago, and once read I put the books aside and went onto other things, other sorts of books that fell out of the categorisation of Surrealism. More and more I felt that this labelling of books and other works of so-called art was an absurdity in itself: too neat, too clean, too easy to pigeonhole or, to use an image concerning the human body, too easy to digest.

I carried on my life outside of reading, and being by nature a solitary sort of person I really only shared my thoughts with myself. I had no special partner and I had no special friends, but one thing I did do; I did categorise myself as being homosexual. I told myself, and I believed, that I only desired my own sex. It was in my dreams that my sexuality took its sharpest form. I encountered other bodies sexually and committed sexual acts that I did not commit during my waking life. In fact my dream life became so piercingly real that often during my waking life I thought my actions while awake were a dream and that my dreams were my real life.

There is little to say about me. I am middle-aged, male, and when I look in a mirror I see a pleasant sort of face looking out at me. I cannot remember how I looked when I was a youth and only have photographs to remind me. The man that looks out of those photographs looks very different from the man whom I see daily in the mirror, and often I have the fantasy that I have been taken over by a completely other face, other form. There seems to me to be no bridge that leads from the youthful man that I was to the man that I am today.

I put this down in passing. It is not particularly relevant to the story I am about to tell. It is, I suppose, what is called background information: details perhaps to evade going into what I see as a particularly humiliating and dreadful incident that happened one afternoon during an exceptionally hot day in May.

I remember waking up badly. I cannot remember the horror of the encounter I had had in my dream that forced me awake, but it took me several hours to shake off the shadow of a memory that clung to me like an invisible cobweb. I drank a lot of tea. I watched an hour of television. I watched image after image of ridiculously unreal people march or wander across the television screen, emitting words that I barely heard, barely understood. They talked about the weather and one man made me laugh. He was standing in a wood outside of Sheffield (the only part of reality that appeared at all real) telling us, the viewers, how beautiful the bluebells looked around him. His feet were firmly planted in the centre of a patch of them. He said that the weather during the early part of the month had been poor, but now as the weather had changed for what he called the better, the bluebells had come out in force. He talked about the possible demise of the English bluebell, apparently due to the invasion of another country's type of bluebell. I cannot remember the country. It may have been Spain. He was relaying this information back to the central studio and the man listening to him there asked him to walk among the bluebells, then to walk into the wood behind. The astonished look on the man's face at this request was amazing to see. For a while he just stood there speechless. Then he uttered a feeble protest about not having been warned about this in advance. I think he even mentioned health and safety, but I cannot be sure that I heard right. And then again the man in the studio asked him to walk away from the bluebells and into the wood.

"It's just a bit of fun," the man in the studio added, as if to encourage him. "It doesn't mean anything."

The response to this was a shuffling of feet in the sea of blue, then an awkward turning to one side: an awkwardness to be associated more with a robot than a man. And then with heavy steps he made a full turn and with his back to the man in the studio, and to those of us who were watching this live performance, he hesitantly stepped forward into the shadows of the wood. A rapid cut to the studio and a rather self-satisfied smile on the face of the man in the studio. I at once turned off the television. This *is* man, I told myself, then with equal awkwardness I got off the sofa and went to make myself breakfast. At last, sure that I was out of the bad dream that had awoken me, and feeling very tired, I ate my cereal and then decided to dress and go to the bank.

The sun beat down as I walked along the street. My bank was a few blocks away and I walked slowly. As I walked a voice inside of me said, you are not awake, you are not awake. This is still the dream, still the nightmare. I stood for a moment and shook off the thoughts. I literally shook them off with my whole body as a dog would shake itself free from persistent but determined fleas. As I was doing this I was conscious of people around me, stopping to stare. Let them look, I thought. I have a right, within reason, to do what I want in the street. I will not be a slave to their absurd conventions.

After what appeared to be a very long time I reached my bank. I remember looking up at the façade of the red brick building, noticing again the gargoyles looking down at me from the top of the roof. They had always struck me as being peculiar: a whim from an architect back in the 1930s, determined to leave his specific trace on an otherwise routine and rather mediocre example of architecture.

"You look particularly malevolent today," I said aloud to them, then lowered my eyes and walked into the darkened interior of the building.

A young man whom I had never seen before approached me. His face was sweaty with the heat and he was wearing a suit that seemed too large for his rather slim body.

"What can I do for you?" he asked.

Normally I went to a cashier at the back of the room, but in the obscurity (why hadn't they turned on more lights?) I could neither make out the cashier nor the glass cage behind which they presided.

"I would like to deposit some money," I said to the young man. "Could you please show me where the cashier is? Somehow it seems very dark in here today."

The young man did not reply to this request, but instead pointed to a chair and asked me to sit down. As I obeyed him a conflicting thought ran through my mind that I should leave the bank at once. This was followed by another thought that I was curious to know what would happen next.

"What is your name?" he asked, standing over me.

I gave him my name, followed by my address, which had not been requested, and after writing down the information on a scrap of paper that he had taken from his pocket he turned around and walked away from me.

"This is not the normal procedure," I said aloud, and as I did so a dark haired woman passed my chair. In the feeble light I could see she was distraught. She was openly crying and her companion, who was much younger than she, was roughly pushing her forwards towards the door and the street.

"I didn't do anything," I heard her cry.

"Don't make such an exhibition of yourself, Edith. Haven't you done enough?"

She cried out again, almost screaming, followed by garbled words that I could not understand, but the man took no notice of her and continued to push her roughly forward. Soon they were lost in the glare of the bright spring light that blazed savagely into us at the opening of the door. Then the door was shut and the vast room was obscurely darkened again.

"I have verified your name and address."

The sweaty young man stood over me. The scrap of paper upon which he had written the information was scrunched up in his hand. He looked disagreeable and his voice was harsh. I stood up and the distance between us being so small, I could smell the fetid breath that came out of his mouth.

"I simply want to put some money into my account," I replied. "Will you or won't you take me to the cashier?"

"No."

The word came out sharp and clear.

"May I ask why?"

My voice was shaking with anger, but instinct told me to suppress it and I tried to be polite. I remained close to him, despite the smell that came from his body, and he in his turn made no move to turn away. We remained like this, glaring at each other in the semi-light.

"We can't accept your money," he said at last.

"Again, may I ask why?"

"You really need to know?" he replied. There the sound of open contempt in his voice.

"If there is anything wrong in this situation, then of course I want to know," I said.

"We are Christians here," he murmured slowly, enunciating each word with the precision of a surgical knife.

"But this is a bank!"

"Yes and no. It is a Christian bank. It is my job to vet all who come through these doors."

I laughed then. I laughed straight into his horrible mean thin face. He smiled at my laugh, then with the same slowness as before said, "You are a masturbator. You can't stop masturbating, and it is on our list as something we cannot accept or respect. You are no longer a client here."

"And what of my money?"

"What money? You have no account here any more. It has been wiped out. Wiped clean."

I ran from him then. I ran inwards into the building and at the place where the cashiers' glass cage used to be there was instead a tiered row of long benches. Row upon row of men and women stared down at me in the gloom.

"Who are you?" I cried aloud at them.

"We are not you."

They cried out in unison, sang it out as if it was the last line of a dreadful religious chorus.

"And what if I am Christian too?" I shouted back at them. "What if my belief is in a different place than this place? What if I am simply a believer in the dream of Christ. Simple and beyond all this."

"There can be no difference."

The chorus sang back their words as if it was a protracted, torn apart *amen*. Then they slowly got up from their seats and descending from the benches, one by one, filed past me.

I was alone in the tomb of the bank. I made my way to the closed door, opened it, and felt the rush of heat upon my body.

Walking back to the flat where I lived I tried not to look at those around me. I felt despised and rejected and alone. And above all, I had to wake up. I had to shake off this ultimate dream that with dreadful clarity I knew to be the dream of life itself. And all the while, the sun hammered nails of light into my face.

BRIGHTON DARKNESS

It was like an operation that had to be undergone. He threw aside the polite American gay novel he had been reading, and turned instead to that monster in the corner of the room that had been awaiting him: the internet. He found the profile of the man easily. In fact he had been stalking him for quite some time.

How are you?

The words appeared in a bubble on the screen. He tapped his reply.

I am well.

Good.

Why is it good?

Shows you have no illness to detract from the experience.

You don't know that.

No, I don't. But I get impressions of people.

He laughed at himself as he replied.

I have met a psychic.

We have not met at all. Yet.

That's true. So how can you say 'good' when you don't know

if I am telling the
truth?

      I told you. I get
      impressions of people.

I may have cancer.
Or something else.

      What something else?

It's true, I am well.
Totally physically
well.

      Good.

There was now a long pause in this encounter of two people who had never met.

   I don't know what to
   say.

      You contacted me. That
      means you are
      considering…

He stared at the monster screen, and could not reply to this.

      Am I right?

The words appeared and he looked at them. They seemed to him to be cold, cold and shivering in their void. He felt afraid, and for the briefest of moments wanted to stop.

      Am I right?

The words returned. Either he continued, or he stopped now. He made the decision to continue.

   You are right.
      Good.

The word 'good' filled him with alarm. He did not like the repetition of this word that reminded him there was nothing good in what he was now doing.

I would prefer it if you would not use that word again.

Does it frighten you?

Yes. I don't know why, but yes.

It's alright to be frightened a little. If you are frightened too much it means you do not want what I have to offer. That is not alright. But be frightened a little.

He replied by tapping in:

Did you use the word 'alright' instead of 'good'? Is it a substitute word?

What are you? A psychiatrist?

A long pause.

My name is Ed.

Your real name?

Does it matter?

Is it the name you want me to call you if we meet?

*Yes, but my name
is Ed. Edward. I
see no reason to give
a fake name.*

        Phil.

Yes.

        You don't believe me?

*Is it the name I would
call you if we met?*

        Why not?

*But it is not your real
name. Is it?*

        I didn't say it was.

Pause.

*I live in Brighton.
Where do you live?*

        I'd rather not say.

Not even if we meet?

        No.

Why?

        It's the way I work.

*You consider this
work?*

Long pause.

        Are you a psychiatrist?

*No. I worked in
marketing. Until the
firm went bust.*

        I understand.

Good!

        *You see! It's a good
word to use. One of my*

favourites.

Phil?

Yes?

What are the terms?

I come to where you live. I remain anonymous. You know nothing about me or my life.

I see. I mean I don't see. Why?

I like to feel guilty about what I do. It gives me pleasure. I like to know the person I'm going to infect. But I want to be anonymous.

These are the terms?

Yes.

A very long pause.

Do you want to go through with it?

Yes, Phil.

That's alright then.

You can say good.

Good.

Just one intimate question.

What?

Why does it give you pleasure?

That's a long story.

Please say.

It's a rotten world. It gives me pleasure to know I may be responsible for getting someone out of it. It's the nearest that comes to murder.

You want to feel it is a crime?

I didn't say that.

You infer it.

Look Mr Psychiatrist.

Ed.

Enough.

Enough questions?

About my motives, yes.

Pause.

How long have you had the virus?

I don't want to put that down.

Why?

It's an intimate question. I replied to one. I do not want to reply to two.

Don't you want to know why I want to be positive?

I don't usually ask.

But would you like to know?

Not particularly. In fact it might diminish my

pleasure. No one gets pleasure out of knowing the person they may kill wants it too much. I said, it's alright, in fact very alright, to be a little afraid. I would prefer it if you were a little afraid of what you seem to want.

I don't SEEM to want it, Phil, I DO want it.

But you are a little afraid of it, aren't you?

He tapped in the word 'yes', concerned that Phil might disappear if he admitted he was not afraid at all.

How old are you Phil?

Does it matter?

Is that too much of a personal question?

I'm 29.

And?

And what? I'll be 30 in 4 months if that adds anything to it.

Physically are—

He stopped. Was he really going to ask this man who had one purpose for him, how he looked physically? The question was in his mind and he sensed that Phil knew it.

I don't think it matters what I look like. How

tall I am, or if I am
marked by illness or
not. Do you think it
matters? Anyway, I'm
not here for my looks.

He did not reply to this.

Have I offended you?

The words looked odd on the screen. They looked out of place, implying manners and feeling. They implied caring, and he knew that Phil should not and would not care about him.

No.

The word was suitably brief.

I don't believe you.

The words hit back. The words suggested an intimation of feeling that neither of them ought really to feel.

Phil, I am not offended.
I am OK to look at.
OK?

The words were defiant. He realised that this was as near to intimacy as he could go. Any more prying or asking, or being the psychiatrist would only alienate. And he did not want to alienate. He was looking for infection, not love.

How soon can we meet?

He had to be business-like. This was a transaction. Phil

was coming to deliver the goods. That was all, and he needed
to know when and at what time.

> *I am more or less free*
> *whenever you want.*

> *I can't ask how near*
> *you are to me, can I?*

Pause.

> *Stupid question. You*
> *already said you didn't*
> *want to tell me.*

> *Brighton as well.*

> *That's good. Thanks*
> *for breaking a rule*
> *about where you are.*

Long pause.

> *You really sure you*
> *want to go through*
> *with it?*

He had no idea what to reply to this comment, so he just
said, yes. He literally said 'yes' as he tapped in the word.

> *Yes.*

Then he gave his full name and address.

> *I can be there any day*
> *this week, except*
> *Saturday.*

> *Thursday?*

> *Thursday is good.*

What time?

2pm?

Yes. You live alone?

Does it matter?

I am asking. Do you live alone?

Yes. Completely alone. Not even a dog or a cat.

It's just this should be completely private. It's essential for me.

I thought I'd ask some friends round to watch.

Sarcastic.

I'm sorry. Just a bit nervous.

I like that. Makes me feel good you feeling nervous. Makes it more…

More what?

Pleasurable.

He wanted to ask if the sex itself would be pleasurable, but knew this was territory he could not go into. He realised Phil's idea of pleasure probably did not depend upon the act of sex itself.

Do you want to ask anything else?

He did want to ask whether Phil wanted to know what he looked like, or what he liked to do sexually, but he knew the answer would be no. Phil was delivering, that was all.

Nothing more.

Until Thursday?

Yes.

He turned off the computer. He was alone in the room. Looking around him, he suddenly felt not only alone, but lonely. The chat or talk or conversation or whatever you could call it, had exhausted him. And yet, despite the exhaustion he was sorry that the screen was blank and that the words that had connected him with this stranger had gone.

"Stupid," he said aloud, and getting up from the chair, stretched.

Outside the sun was shining. It was a hot summer's day, and he wondered whether, if he had chosen to sit in the garden instead, and read the stupid American novel through to the end, he would have given in to the compulsion to contact Phil.

"I might not have given in to the impulse," he said aloud, but then added that if it had not been this afternoon, it would have been some other time. Eventually he would have done the thing he wanted to do.

"I have been considering this often for a while now."

He stopped talking aloud. It was absurd to talk aloud. He was thirty-six, not in his dotage. Thirty-six year old people should not make a habit of talking to themselves. I have friends, he thought. Then he counted them. There was Steve, his best friend. They went to nightclubs together and had a laugh, and Steve had been very supportive after Jason's death. Then there was Sue, who was married. They shared college memories and met often. That made two, and two is a lot of friends to have in this world that is so meagre with its friendship handouts.

He rang Steve.

"Hi, it's me."

"Hello, you."

The same familiar, intimate patter. A million miles away

from the words he had shared on his computer.

"I just wanted to hear a human voice," he said lamely.

"What? No proposition? It's the weekend for fuck's sake. Don't you want to go out?"

"I was reading this really inane book and it depressed me, so I just wanted to hear a voice."

"Thanks! You make it sound like any voice would do."

It was the truth.

"No, Steve, don't be silly."

"So what shall we do then?"

"Not out. I don't want to go out."

"I'll come round. I'll bring some beers. And a new DVD I know you'll like. Okay?"

Suddenly it was not okay. He had just rung Steve to hear a human voice. He did not want to go out with him this weekend. Neither did he want him round for the evening. As much as he felt a sense of loneliness, he knew that Steve, as much as he loved him, would not be able to fill it.

"I rang because I just wanted to talk. Hear a voice. Sorry, *your* voice."

"That's all?"

"That's all."

"Well, what do you want to talk about?"

"Oh, how your week has been. What your office has been up to. Normal things."

"I could come over and do that."

He knew he was being unkind and that Steve was as alone as he was. This was friendship, after all, and shouldn't he give a little? He mumbled into the phone that he wouldn't cook dinner, but that if Steve was willing to come over with a take-away, he would be welcome.

"You mean it?"

Steve was like some big, lumbering, over-eager dog, and he could imagine his tail wagging with pleasure.

"What's the DVD?" he asked.

"*Black Swan.*"

"But it's got horror," he said.

"You like horror. I've seen it twice. Would you prefer me to bring something else?"

"No, bring that. I just read some mixed reviews."

"Don't believe all you read. It's the director who made— oh hell, I can't remember what he made now, but we liked it. Just forget it's about ballet."

"I hate ballet."

"Yes, Ed, I know."

The evening went well. The take-away was Chinese and good, and Steve had brought a bottle of wine. Afterwards they sat down side by side on the sofa and watched the film. He didn't like it, but lied to please Steve. If nothing else, the acting had been good.

"You look sad," Steve said.

Ed looked at his friend. Steve was never sad as such, and this was why they got on so well. He was a total opposite. He was also physically attracted to Steve, but had never told him.

"It's been a rough week," he said.

"Not having a job?"

"That too."

"You mean Jason?"

He said yes, because it was true. For weeks he had had vivid dreams about his dead lover. In the dreams he had seen him again, contorted with pain, and angry that he was dying. Jason had screamed his anger at fate to the last.

"I'm sleeping really badly. I see him almost every night."

Steve reached out a big friendly hand and placed it on his shoulder.

"He died so—"

He stopped.

"Yes, I know," Steve said. "I was there. Remember?"

Most people hadn't been there, and even if they had been, they would not have wanted to see it: the emaciated limbs and the vacant look of Jason's blind eyes. The solid core truth of an AIDS death.

"I miss him so much," Ed said.

He turned to look at Steve and noticed that he looked sombre and unhappy. He knew it was unfair of him to inflict these memories on his best friend.

"It's been over two years now," he said, "and I should be getting over the worst of it. But the worst of it is, I'm not. It also isn't right that I keep inflicting it on you. Over and over again. I'm sorry."

Steve squeezed his shoulder in support, then got up and poured them both a glass of wine.

"My fault," he said. "*Black Swan* was the last thing you needed."

"It could have been worse. It could have been the Coen brothers."

They both laughed at that, and changed the conversation.

"So are you seeing anybody?"

Steve shrugged his shoulders in reply and gulped down his wine.

"I take that to mean you don't want to tell me, and I may add, it's not good to drink a fine wine that way."

"Listen to who's being posh," Steve said.

"Well, are you seeing anybody?" Ed insisted.

"I went to the club this week. It was so fucking boring, but I was feeling horny, and there was this Italian guy from Milan or somewhere. I made the mistake of going to bed with him."

"Why was it a mistake?"

Steve looked at first as if he wanted to avoid answering this, then blurted out, "He didn't want sex with a condom, the stupid, bloody bastard. I kicked him out of bed and told him to go find a fucking taxi."

"I'm sorry," Ed said.

"It's not as if he was young," Steve continued. "He was in his forties. Should've known bloody better. I really wanted to kill him."

When Ed heard Steve say that, he suddenly started to laugh

and thought he would be unable to stop. He saw himself at the computer that afternoon. The memory was brutally absurd.

"What are you laughing about?" Steve asked.

"Nothing. It's so—so ridiculous."

He laughed and he laughed. He stood up, almost choking with laughter. Steve came over and shook him by the shoulders.

"Are you taking the mickey out of me or what?"

In moments of confusion and dismay, Steve's Irish accent came out. It sounded very bright and very strong, and Ed stopped laughing.

"You sound as if you come from Dublin," he said.

"I do. What's so original about that?"

"I just—"

But he did not finish the sentence. Steve was holding him in his arms and he allowed himself to be held. He was shorter than Steve, and standing, he came up to Steve's shoulder. He buried his head into Steve's broad neck like a frightened small animal.

"I'm a fool," he muttered.

"What?"

He heard Steve's voice as if from far away, and when he raised his head to look at him, he kissed him on the mouth. His first impulse was to pull away, feeling suddenly that he shouldn't have done that, but Steve held him hard against him.

"I shouldn't have done that," he said.

"Why?"

"It's not what we do," he replied.

"Then we should try to do it a bit more often. I've never used my Irish accent on you so strongly before. I've been wondering for a long time what I could do to make you—"

"Make me what?" Ed replied.

"Love me," Steve said simply.

He kissed Steve again and they made their way to the bedroom. Steve was gentle and the sex was full of the thing that Ed needed most, and that was kindness.

"I never thought it would ever happen."

Steve lay back on the bed and stared away from Ed. Ed could tell he was frightened that what they had done was going to spoil their friendship. He reached over and touched Steve.

"You saved me," he said.

"What?"

There was a laugh in Steve's voice as he turned round and faced Ed. Ed, with a shock of surprise, realised how much he had meant by what he had just said.

"Who or what have I saved you from?" Steve asked.

"From doing the worst thing that anyone could do, that's all."

Steve laughed again.

"Oh, Ed, you are—"

To stop him from saying what he was, Ed kissed Steve on the mouth.

"Tell me tomorrow morning," he said.

They spent the weekend in bed. Ed delighted in discovering that he was in love with Steve, and that he had been in love with him for a long time. Also for the first time in weeks, he slept well, and there were no nightmare visions of Jason and the agony he had gone through. It was during the early hours of Monday morning that Ed told Steve what he had committed himself to.

"But why?" Steve asked.

"I read a bad book and it depressed me. And instead of ringing you as I should have done, I contacted this man."

"Don't be flippant," Steve said sternly. "I really want to know why."

"Let's talk over a cup of coffee."

Under the harsh bright light of the kitchen, sitting at the kitchen table, Ed tried to explain why he had gone to that site.

"I wanted to die the way Jason died," he said. "I wanted to

go through what he went through. I felt it was the only way to get through the grief and the nightmares. To go where he went: to the extreme of what a human being can bear."

He looked over at Steve. Steve's face was drawn and tired. He looked much older than his thirty odd years.

"It's hard to understand. It's as if I was in the grip of a sort of madness. I could say it was a madness induced by loneliness, by a sense of loss for him. But I honestly do not know the real cause."

"And now that you know I'm in love with you?" Steve asked.

Ed could no longer control himself and burst into tears. He felt ashamed. Ashamed of what he had intended to do with his body, and strangely ashamed that Steve could still love him knowing that.

"I wanted to get infected," he said. "It's not an exaggeration, Steve. It's what I really believed I wanted. I'm not even sure the impulse won't return. The need for destruction must still be there. Deep down, it must still be there, despite the fact that I love you as well."

Steve came over and cradled him, as a protective parent would cradle a frightened and confused child.

"I was there with you in that hospital," he said quietly. "What we saw was terrible and it will never leave us. I smile and bury the memory, but believe me, I have not forgotten. His death was like some terrible passion: a sort of crucifixion. No one with any feeling could not cry out against that. It is everything that I loathe in nature. The inherent cruelty. The passion that never ends for so many. How the world can absorb all that terror and pain I do not understand. And there is no way I can believe it is justified under any natural law. Yet at the same time I have to acknowledge that, justifiable or not, it exists. It is the extremity of everything that is most appalling about life, and dearest Ed, it is not for you to wish it upon yourself."

"I know."

That was all he could say. He put his arms around Steve. The bright light fell upon them both: the bright light of the morning, and he was glad of it. He was glad now that the dark nightmare seemed to be over.

Two days later he received a message. It was not from Phil, but a friend of Phil's. It said in the briefest of words that Phil had been taken ill, that he was in hospital and that he would be unable to keep his appointment for Thursday.

THE VISITOR

I am weary of waiting. I long for the door to open, to hear again the sound of the voice that says, "Look, here I am. I have come to stay and to talk once more." Instead, I turn back to the book I have been reading. I re-join the characters who are fictions, who have always been fiction to the legion of readers who have encountered their world before me. I take up their story, and re-enter the lie that is their lives, using my tired eyes to follow every twist of plot and every utterance of dialogue. But then at last, my eyes are sore with reading. I put the book down and stare at the closed door.

"It is enough,"

I get up and walk around the room. I am familiar with every object in it. I look at the books piled high by the black chair where I have been sitting. I glance at the old fireplace, open and ready for a fire that I never light. The fireplace has been in this room since the house was built in 1907. It has all its original features, and I wonder sometimes at how many people put coals in its grate before I came to live here. It is easier for me to turn on a fan heater plugged into the wall. All I have to do is turn a dial on the front of it for warmth. No need to bend down, put on wood or coals and set a match. For a start, it is difficult for me to bend, and then a fire that is real, always needs attention: needs a sort of love in fact to keep it going.

"Who will keep me going?"

I talk aloud to myself. I have done it for quite a few years now. I hear my voice, and very occasionally I have the illusion that it is not me talking, but someone else. This is a comfort to me. I talk in the hope that I will forget it is my voice, but it is only when I cease to wait, cease to expect, that

I have the illusion of hearing another.

"You are a fool."

I walk around the room several times, then I go out into the hall and turn to face the narrow stairs that lead upwards to the bedrooms. I only go up these stairs when it is eventually time to go to bed. I know every room up there, and conveniently there is a second toilet downstairs, so I do not even have that excuse to go up. All the same, I have a ritual of leaving the living room that runs the whole length of the house, of going into the hall, and standing there, staring up the stairs.

"Why are you so silent up there?"

I often call up. It is part of the ritual. I like to call out for someone, and my hand reaches for the bannister as I stare with fixed eyes at the empty path upwards.

"Well, if you don't want to reply, then don't. I don't care if you choose to be silent."

My voice is petulant and accusing. I want to make the person I am calling out to feel guilty that he has remained quiet for so long, and then I wait, holding on for a good five or ten minutes. Sometimes I can become quite lost in waiting for a reply and really do believe that someone, anyone, will call back down to me. But eventually I turn away, walk down the hallway to the front door and, opening it for a moment, look out at the overgrown path that leads to the gate.

"I really must get the garden done," I say, and look at the density of green weed and the brightness of a wild flower.

"How yellow it is," I murmur.

All my wild flowers are yellow. I name them yellow, even if they are not. Yellow is my favourite colour and I see it even when it is not there. My eye ignores the red, the mauve, or the blue. I look at the flowers, fighting for life among the weeds and I repeat to myself that I must get a gardener, but I know that somehow I will fail to do so.

Once back in the living room I sit down again and try to read from where I left off. But soon my eyes really fail me and I have to put the book down.

"It's not my concentration," I say, "but my eyes. My eyes are worn out. How long will it be before I go blind?"

This is one of my worst fears. I have had it all my life. As a child I would scream if I woke up in the night to find myself in the dark. To be in the dark is close to a premature burial. Both fears I had as a child, and throughout my life they have haunted me. Even after the events of my life brought me to this house, this neat house in Brighton, there has been no peace from them. You will go blind and die here, and maybe death will not be death and they will bury you alive in your coffin. In various places in the house I write notes, putting them beside my reading chair or by my bed, asking anyone who finds me to have me cremated.

"I will be blind in the box when they put me into the fire," I say. "Will I even then feel the pain of the flames?"

It is like this that I am tortured during my days.

Oh how weary I am of waiting. How I long for the door to open, to hear again the sound of the voice that says, "Look, here I am. I have come to stay and to talk once more." But who is he exactly that I wait for? My mind is confused and there is only a jumble of mixed up faces in my memory. And anyway, what voice could sound familiar, when I have forgotten who I am waiting for?

I close the day by making an early meal. I steam my food: mostly vegetables as I have never really enjoyed the taste of meat. I stand in the middle of the kitchen and eat my meal. I have been sitting most of the day, and during this (almost) last act of the day I like to stand and look out of the kitchen window. Summer of course is best for this as the window faces west and I can watch the sun sink, or when it is cloudy, watch the light fade. As the kitchen fades into darkness I say a prayer to a God that I do not believe in to let me keep my sight—this above all, to keep my sight, to see another day.

Usually I am restless in bed. I wake up several times in the night. My bedside light is always on, but I get up and put the main light on, and sitting in my bed, resume my reading. For a few hours I am lost in another world than my own. But then at last, tiredness pulls me back into sleep and I get a few more hours before it is time to get up.

This is surprisingly easy. I am quite punctual with my morning hours. By eight I have finished in the bathroom. I always have a long bath and make sure that I am shaved and that my hair is neatly combed.

"How lucky you are," I say to myself, "to still have a full head of hair."

In the past, people always said what nice hair I had. I smile at myself in the mirror. I see the smile, but not the rest of my face. I avoid the rest of my facial features. I only look once, after I have combed my hair. There is no chance of me catching myself unawares in a mirror elsewhere in the house, as I only possess the small one above the sink in the bathroom. I am not sure why the smile is necessary, but the fact that I do it every morning, makes it so. Perhaps it is the smile of another person I am seeing there.

"What a fool you are," I say again, "with all these conjectures."

Well, I have set out my nights and my days, and now it is time to recall that day, that one day that broke the ritual. The rupture of my solitude did not last long, but long enough and significant enough for me to narrate it back to myself.

"But aren't you creating a novel?" I say to myself. "It is a lie after all."

Then I repeat to myself that whatever it was, it must be said. The door did at last open, and someone did come in.

It was an autumn day. About eleven in the morning. Quite suddenly the front door bell rang. My first reaction was one of fear: supposing it was one of those teenagers who lived a few doors down from me. They had seen me once at the gate to the house, and had laughed as they passed by. As they entered their own house, one of them had shouted, "Go fuck yourself," before slamming their door. This had happened quite a long time ago, but the pressing of the doorbell sounded so aggressive, it reminded me of them.

"It could be the woman next door," I say. "She sometimes rings. Don't you remember? It was only last week she rang the bell to make sure you were alright. Maybe this time she wants to borrow something."

I get up from my chair and go to the hallway. The wood of the door is momentarily threatening. Inside me a voice tells me not to answer, not to open, but another voice adds that I am not yet mad. Not yet. And so I open the door, and there on the mat outside, a tall young man stands, facing me.

"Hello," he says simply.

I stare at him in silence, not replying.

"You don't remember me, do you?"

I shake my head, and he reaches out to shake me by the hand. Automatically, my own hand reaches out and clasps his.

"I am Michel," he says.

Michel. The name jostles inside my head with all the other names I have known in my lifetime. I cannot remember a Michel.

"You used to call me Michael."

His voice is soft and gentle, and suddenly like the last piece in a particularly difficult jigsaw puzzle, the memory of him fits into place. Of course I know him. He is a friend, I say to myself, and a welcome one. Now you need no longer be weary of waiting.

"Come in," I say.

He steps into the house, and I make a gesture with my hand for him to go along the hall first.

"The living room is untidy," I add.

He laughs the laugh I now remember, and says quietly that my rooms have always been untidy.

"I was constantly tidying up after you," he says.

Coming from him, these are not words of rudeness. How could they be in someone so close to me who has come to stay, who has come to break the silence with words?

"I came by Eurostar," he says. "Then the train from St Pancras."

He smiles and sits down in my chair. He picks up the book I have been reading, looks at the cover very quickly, then puts it down again. I stand awkwardly in the middle of the room, not knowing what to say next. I want to say, help me Michael. Help me, please, because I have been alone for so long and I am not used to this.

"It's quiet here," he observes.

"Like the grave," I say, and we both laugh. Then I shudder as I mentally see a group of people shovelling earth onto my coffin. I want to cry out for them to stop. No, you must not do this, I want to say, but I am alone in the dark and stifling. I hammer on wood, and then the final blackness overtakes me.

Struggling from this all too vivid vision I ask him if I can make him a meal, make him something to drink.

"Some English tea would be fine," he says. "I ate on the train on the way to London."

"It must have been only a sandwich," I said. "What else do they do these days?"

He smiles and nods his head, but adds that it was a good sandwich and that he had two. He then goes on to describe the fillings in the sandwich as I prepare the tea in the kitchen. He does not join me there, but sits in my chair and looks around the room as he chatters on.

"I like it here," he says finally. "I like to see you with all your things around you."

"A lifetime of things," I say.

"But good. Solid," he insists. "I especially remember the pictures. You had so many friends who were artists. Ah, yes, the portrait of yourself, by that now famous man. What is his name?"

I cannot remember, and tell him so. I also remark that the picture is unsigned, so for the time being, and perhaps for always, the name will be forgotten.

"Well, the portrait looks like you," he says.

"Did."

"No. It does. Still."

The tea is made and I take it into him. He has now got up from the chair and is standing at the bay window, looking at the jungle outside.

"This really needs doing," he says, and it is then that I ask him how long he is going to stay. He either does not hear my question, or pretends not to, for he makes no reply. Sensing that there is perhaps a good reason for this, I go up to him and hand him the tea. He takes it from me, smiles, then drinks it down in one long gulp.

"Not the English way of drinking tea," he mocks gently as he returns the cup to me. "Not something Virginia Woolf would have done."

"I am reading her now," I say.

"Yes. I saw the cover. *The Years*."

I feel suddenly ashamed, as if he has caught me in an embarrassing act. I want to cover my traces. I do not want him to think that I only read books like this. But what are books like this? I ask myself. Narrow books, the voice responds in my head. What the world calls feminine books. Books that focus on the particular, on the detail, and not on the broad canvas. I want to tell him that I am capable of appreciating the broad canvas and that the last book I read was a re-reading of Tolstoy. But then again, that would have been a lie. The last novel I read had been an obscure work by an obscure woman writer who was only remembered for just one book.

"I read a lot," I say. "You must not judge me by one book."

"And all those French authors?" he asks. "Do you still read them?"

I shake my head. I want to say the past is the past, but how can I when he is standing there.

He moves out into the centre of the room. I watch as he bends down to look through the pile of CDs on the floor.

"Ah," he says at last and brings out a CD of French

popular songs from the 1960s.

"May I?" he asks, and before I can answer, he puts the CD on. He gets up, comes towards me, and before I can resist, takes me in his arms. Rather clumsily, we dance cheek to cheek in the living room. The touch of his body against mine is both beautiful and terrifying: beautiful because it is so right and so familiar, terrifying because an insistent voice in my head tells me to back away and to tell him to go.

"Do you remember those nights?" His voice whispers in my ear.

"Yes," I say.

"The name of the club? Do you remember the name?"

"*La Boîte à Chansons*," I reply.

"Right."

He laughs his familiar chuckling laugh.

"I first met you by falling at your feet. It was winter and I had slippery shoes. I slipped and fell down the stairs, holding a statue of the Virgin Mary."

The song on the CD stops and is replaced by a harsher sound. It is impossible to dance closely to this music and we break away. He stands and looks at me. His dark brown hair is dishevelled and has fallen over his eyes. I tell him he is looking at me through a curtain.

"So I am," he replies and gracefully flicks the curtain of hair back.

"The statue didn't break," I say, not wanting to relinquish the memories he has awoken in me. "We spent a long time at the bottom of those stairs examining it."

"It came from a small church in the Vosges," he says. "I had been there for a winter holiday, and I am not ashamed to say that I stole it from a deserted church."

Then we are not talking any more. He has taken me by the hand, and leading me as if he knows the house, takes me upstairs to the main bedroom. We undress in silence, and I stare at his young naked body in dismay. I want to cry out, how can it be this young? How can it be this firm and strong?

Then I look down at my own withered limbs, at my own distressed flesh. I stare above all at the wrinkled stomach that bears the mark of a recent operation. I run my finger over the mark on my flesh and tell myself that this is what time has done.

"I am—"

He stops me by putting a finger to his lips, gesturing for silence. I obey him and lie on the bed, watching as his young and sexually eager body seeks mine. His pressing against me produces pain as much as pleasure. His flesh is too heavy, and mine is too frail, and when he enters me I scream out. My mind goes dark and my breath begins to fail. Oh God, I cry out inside, is this the onset of death? But soon there is release. He ejaculates, and at the moment of climax, we separate. I can breathe once more.

"That was exactly as it used to be," he says quietly.

We lie side by side, not touching any more.

"But I have been unfaithful," he murmurs.

I do not want to know to who, but he tells me all the same.

"That is one of the reasons I came here. I know it sounds as if I just wanted to use you, but really, I don't mean it like that. You were the only person I wanted to turn to. The only important person I could turn to."

"I understand," I reply, not understanding at all. Inside I feel a stab of jealousy and anger. Why does it have to be like this? I want to ask. Why has it always been like this? It was jealousy and anger and emotional pain that made me become a recluse, that finally drove me back to this place. You, Michael, or Michel, are part of that process, that inevitable process that led me back.

"We should not have—"

I am speaking aloud, but I cannot finish the sentence. How can I define what we have just done, or even attempt to give it a name? My flesh is too old to speak of this in terms of making love or having sex. The old have something else when their flesh touches another, but there is no picture in words that I can give for it.

"I am old now," I say simply.

"What has that got to do with it?" he asks, raising himself up on an arm and looking down at my face.

"I am Michael, remember," he says. "With me, there is no age. Can we not agree on that? Our flesh is too familiar to be defined by years."

"At least I can talk to you," I say.

The words startle me, for they are painfully true. I want to say that my solitude has invented this, but I cannot spoil his reality. I want to say that he is a phantom, but how can I deny the firmness of his flesh and the sensation I felt as his penis entered me? I affirm this. I affirm his presence, but above all I affirm his voice that has broken down the wall of my silence. He has come to stay and to talk once more, and that is enough.

"So what happened to make you come to me?" I ask.

"A boy. Isn't it always that?"

He sighs, turns away, and lies once again at my side.

"His name was Pavel, or so he said."

"Not French?"

"No, Czech. He had just returned from the fighting in Prague. He had a few wounds from that useless battle against the Russians."

Inside me a voice is saying, stop, this is history, and is best forgotten, but I do not want to interrupt him. I know he needs to talk, and after all, I need to hear his voice.

"Wenceslas Square. The youth burning himself in protest. He explained it all so clearly, so vividly, and I believed him."

"So there was a lie?" I questioned.

"Isn't there always a lie?"

He starts to cry, and it is my turn to bend over and look at his face. His features are contorted with pain, and he has thrust a fist into his open mouth. The sexual act between us was not a climax, but this is. This is what he has come to me for: to finally, and once and for all, cry it all out. I reach for his arm and gently withdraw the fist from his mouth. I expect a scream to come but none does. He cries and cries, but he does not scream out. I know that he wants to, but he is regaining control over himself.

"I was in love with him," he says. "The only boy I have ever really loved like that."

Again the anger and the jealousy hitting hard inside me. The voice in my brain says, why must we always be carriers of distress, why must we always take the emotional blood and spill it onto others?

"He was not Czech," he says. "He lived with me for weeks with this lie, imitating perfectly a Czech accent, describing in minute detail the arrival of the Russians and what they did to his people and I believed him. I believed everything."

He paused, his voice breathless.

"Then I felt the full brunt of the truth. I woke up one day to find him gone. He had taken all my money, and he had gone. For nights I asked about him in the bars of Paris. I even returned to *La Boîte à Chansons* where we had first met, hoping that someone may have seen him. I believed then that he was a criminal, and that that place would be the last place he would return to. But I was wrong. The night after he left me, he was seen there, going off with another man. The man he went off with was pointed out to me. Someone I too had slept with once. The man told me that Pavel's real name was Tom and that he was an American, working his way through Europe and seeing the sights; that he was collecting enough money to return home to the States."

"It happens a lot," I say sadly, having heard this kind of story so often before. A long, long time ago.

"No, don't say that."

"Michael, we learn," I whisper. "Eventually we learn."

"I don't ever want to learn."

His voice is the dull, denying voice of a child who will not allow its illusions to be destroyed.

"But that does not mean I'm not sorry," I add. "I feel your

sorrow. Truly."

He gets up off the bed and puts on his clothes. He goes downstairs to the kitchen and I hear him making a cup of tea. I hear the kettle boil and the water pouring into a cup. I even hear him stirring sugar into the cup. It is then that I put on my clothes and go down to join him. He is standing at the kitchen window, looking out as the sun sinks.

"I like your garden."

His voice is neutral and he pauses between each small sip from the cup. Then he puts the cup down and says he must go.

"But you have come all this way," I cry.

"I know," he says, "but it is time for me to leave."

"I will never understand," I say.

He looks at me and his eyes are full of tears. Quite suddenly he has the appearance of an old man.

"You're right. We learn. And it is such a trivial story. It is not worth all the tears, and all the pain. He was a worthless boy, and yet I know I will never love in the same way that I loved him."

Now the door closes and he is gone. My younger self has gone, but as the light fades in the room I hope that I will live long enough for him to return once more.

THE HEART

1

"Sometimes I feel that my heart may stop. Stop, simply because it has nowhere to continue to." He paused then added, "My heart goes on, but there is nowhere left. It has a journey to make and yet there is no destination. The destinations were passed long ago, and my heart is conscious that it is without purpose."

Frederick stared at him and said, "But your heart is an organ in your body. It does not think."

"Yes, I know that. But I think for it, and it responds to my thoughts. My heart is central to me, both physically and in all other ways. It knows when the journey has been completed, that all journeys for it have been completed, and that it must stop because it can't just go on: not simply continue for its own sake, which is my sake after all. I am my heart and my heart is me. Whatever it is that commands the physical heart, the heart that beats inside me, will cease when it ceases."

"They say the spirit—"

Andrew made an impatient gesture with his hand.

"Who are they? Others with hearts that they are not truly aware of? Others who do not know how married they are to the organ that beats within them?"

"I don't understand you, Andrew. I am at a loss."

Frederick stood up then and Andrew looked at him. He looked at the tall figure of the man who had once been his lover, but was no more.

"His heart stopped because of us," Andrew said softly.

"He died. It was unexpected."

"A year ago, when all journeys ended for me. Where was he when he died?"

"You know."

"Remind me."

Frederick sat down again and lit a cigarette. He smiled as he held it for a moment in front of him, looking at it.

"They also say this kills," he said.

"Forget them," Andrew replied impatiently. "Tell me how and where he died. No one remembers but you."

Frederick drew on the cigarette and closed his eyes.

"It was without warning," he said.

"You mean his heart stopped?"

"Yes."

"Where did it stop?"

"On a boat. We had sailed down from Venice to Turkey. It was his first time there—"

"—and he chose to go without me," Andrew added, interrupting. "Yes, I know that."

"And you know how he died. Why must I repeat again and again where it was and how it was? This absurd ritual."

"Indulge me," Andrew said.

He stared then at Frederick and he knew that the man who had died on the boat had stopped him from continuing his relationship; his physical relationship with Frederick had been killed by this man's death. Terence.

"Did Terence suffer?" he asked.

"No. He said he felt strange. Nothing more."

"But feeling strange can be suffering in itself. His heart knew that and died."

There was silence between them.

Andrew got up from where he was sitting and said, "It is close in here. May I open the window?"

"Of course."

He got up, brushing against Frederick's chair as he approached the long windows that led out into the garden. Outside it was summer, and the garden was quiet. There was no birdsong, no breath of air.

"I cannot breathe," he said as he stood at the open windows. A long white curtain moved, and he felt it brush against his face. But where had the air come from to move it?

"There is no wind, and yet the curtain moved," he said, "like someone coming in, making it move."

Frederick got up from the chair and came to stand by him. He put a hand on Andrew's shoulder. Andrew shuddered at the touch, and for a moment felt good. It was as if the hand was giving permission to the heart in him to continue, to continue even without a destination.

"How are you?" Frederick asked. "Now. At this moment."

"I won't die," Andrew said. "Not so suddenly. Not like Terence. And yet my heart will still threaten to stop."

He moved forward into the richly flowered garden, and Frederick followed. There was an arbour at the end of the path they were on. They walked to it and sat down in it, side by side. Beyond the arbour, winding its way down to the furthest limit of the garden was the place they called the place of roses. Andrew looked and was amazed at how varied the roses were this year, flaunting their heads in proud confusion, mingling their heads together: like people mingling, but so much more beautiful. He admired the variety of colour, mostly dominant reds and yellows but also others, more faded, as if they were floating Persian carpets, discoloured by age.

"I love this garden," Andrew said. "This garden keeps me alive, Frederick. Do you know that? Have I never told you that?"

"Maybe," Frederick replied. "Maybe you have, but we have said so much to each other, over and over again, like melodies it seems to me, melodies one tries to remember but cannot always."

Andrew laughed.

"The birds have melodies when they sing. I certainly don't have melodies when I speak. Not in my voice anyway. In the mind that dictates the heart maybe, but not in the voice. But where are the birds today? Why do we not hear them?"

"The blackbird's song has left us," Frederick said. He

stood and stretched his arms out as if he wanted to clutch at something, as if he was yearning to touch something that was not there, something Andrew could not see.

"I want—" he began.

"Yes, go on," Andrew said.

"It will be autumn soon. I am afraid of the autumn."

"That was when Terence died," Andrew said quietly.

"I know."

"Why did we let our relationship kill him? And why did he choose to go away, alone with you?"

"Let's walk," Frederick replied, "down the path between the roses. I promised to pick a few for my mother."

They walked, picking out an armful of roses, one by one. Frederick cut his wrist on the thorns and blood trickled down his arm. Andrew looked at the blood, but as Frederick paid no attention to it, neither did he.

2

It was a year ago. Andrew was entering the living room of the house that he shared with Terence. He had just returned from an afternoon spent in bed with Frederick. It had been more of an exercise in the style of loving than loving.

"The sun is sinking between the trees," Terence said as Andrew entered the room.

Andrew looked at Terence, seated in a chair in front of the window. A book lay discarded by the chair, wide open, its pages turning slowly in the early evening breeze.

"Have you been reading all afternoon?" he asked.

Terence turned his head towards him and smiled. He was young, and yet Andrew thought, today he looks old.

"No. I slept most of the time. With the sun on my face. It was good. And you? What did you do?"

Andrew had no desire to talk. He did not want to lie, and yet he knew that he would lie.

"I met up with Tina. Maybe you don't remember Tina."

"No, I don't remember Tina."

Terence laughed. It was a disbelieving laugh. The laughter seemed to say, this woman does not exist at all. Why do you have to invent a woman? Andrew heard this, but he had not lied to that extent. The woman did exist. She was called Tina and she was a librarian he had got friendly with years before. He also had not seen her for years.

"As I don't remember her, we don't need to talk about her," Terence added. "I am happy you had a pleasant time with her. That's all."

"She's—" Andrew began.

"Please. No more needs to be said."

Terence raised his hand high in the air. The gesture looked like an order for Andrew to stop. Andrew was grateful for this silent order and went out of the room into the kitchen. On the wide wooden table, the remains of lunch were still there—a solitary lunch that Terence had had with himself. There was still plenty of food left: a good bottle of wine, half full, to accompany it and half a chicken with salad at the side. Hungrily he ripped some white flesh from the chicken and stuffed it into his mouth. Quickly, as if he was doing something indecent, he washed it down by raising the bottle of wine to his lips. The wine was warm, but the taste was good: a full taste that only added to his hunger. He had not eaten at Frederick's, and he had been there since eleven that morning. He remembered how Terence had asked him if he needed to eat before he went out, and he had said no.

"Taste good?"

Terence stood in the kitchen doorway. He was smiling.

"We had the smallest cake for tea," Andrew lied.

"Then you should have had more."

Terence moved towards the table and began to clear away the remains of the lunch.

"They had run out of food. Too many people before us. You know how it is in summer when you go to these places late in the afternoon."

"No, I don't," Terence said quickly. "Have you forgotten how I have always disliked tea houses? The fuss people make over such trivial food and expensive tea." Then he looked sharply at Andrew and added, "Why do I always have to remind people of things they already know? I seem to spend most of my time repeating facts about myself that I have said many times before. I have come to believe that people just don't listen when you tell them simple facts about yourself."

"Sorry," Andrew said, and moved away from the table. His appetite had quite suddenly gone.

"Please go on eating. It's obvious you are starving."

"An exaggeration, Terence, an exaggeration. I never starve."

He went back into the living room and stood in the centre of it. He felt trapped as if he was in a place without an exit. I can't continue like this, he thought to himself.

He listened to Terence move about in the kitchen. He heard the water running and the sound of the dishes being placed in the sink. He could see, in his mind's eye, Terence up to his elbows in washing-up liquid. He did not know why, but the image made him feel sick. Then he noticed that it had gone quite dark in the room and he went to turn on the lights.

"Can't we stay for a while with the lights off?"

Terence was standing in the kitchen doorway, a tea towel in his hands.

"I have almost finished in there," he added. "Maybe we can sit in the room for a while and watch it get dark."

"As you wish," Andrew said, and sat down. He waited as Terence finished clearing up, and as he waited he recalled a night years before when they had sat in the dark together. Carlos Kleiber. The radio. The second movement of Beethoven's Seventh. The hanging on by a thread: the thread through a needle eye of sound, from one second to another. The sound, fragile and poised to stop, as the heart of the music beats to the conductor's beat, and the orchestra, outside of the conductor, responds. And then? What then as the baton falls and the transmission stops? The music from another place ceases to be. The radio itself is a silent coffin. Only a memory. A memory now as he remembers the night with Terence when they had heard that music.

I was in love then, he says to himself. But I am in love now. Even loving Frederick, as I think I do, I am in love now. The kitchen sounds kill the memory of that once heard music, but all the same, the sounds are good. I must not feel sick at the thought of his hands in the hot water, washing the remains of food from the dishes.

Then Terence is sitting opposite him. There is light enough in the room for them to see each other.

"I can smell the flowers in the garden," Andrew said. "Can you?"

"Not much. I do not have a nose for scents. But you, you love the flowers so much. How is it possible that you can differentiate one flower from another by its smell? It is a mystery to me, and yet it is simple to you. Simple to a lot of people no doubt." He sighed, then added, "I am deficient, no doubt." He paused then for a moment before saying, "Only in Frederick's living room do I smell the roses. He has so many."

It was a shock to Andrew, hearing Terence say Frederick's name. They knew each other. He knew that. In their Brighton circle, everyone knew everyone else, and he should not have been surprised that Terence mentioned his name, but it was the flowers. Terence had noticed the flowers in Frederick's garden. That garden of his was a passion for Andrew that almost exceeded his physical passion for Frederick. He knew he would remember the different colours, forms and smells there long after he had forgotten the tactile memory of Frederick's body, or the contours of his form.

"I love his garden," Andrew said simply. "It is the best I have been in. Not the diversity in it, though it surely has that, but the intensity of it. It goes deep with a single richness."

He smiled, and looked across at Terence who had turned his head away.

"Did you know that Frederick is going to Turkey to buy antiques for his shop?" Terence asked.

"No. I did not know. I have not seen him for a while."

The lie was simple. It hung in the air like a question. How could I have said that, it seemed to ask. Why could I not have simply said that I did not know, which I don't, and have left it at that? Why this necessity to always not speak the truth?

"When is he going?" he added, not wanting to ask how Terence knew something that he did not know.

"Next month."

These two words made Andrew relax. Four weeks is a long time in a relationship in its first flush. No doubt in this first flush of passion there had been no time to mention such a detail. He saw himself in bed with Frederick that afternoon and understood how in the silence between the excess of lust and the quiet of tenderness there would have been no active thought of this journey.

"I don't like Turkey," he said, and got up to get himself a drink. He poured himself a glass of whisky, but deliberately did not ask Terence if he wanted some. He wanted to be cruel to Terence, and this was a small cruelty of rudeness and avoidance that was easy to make. Heavily, he sat back down in his chair. The light was now fading fast in the room, and without asking he turned on the reading light by his chair. The sudden brightness was harsh. Terence made a startled sound as if the trivial brutality of it had hurt, and Andrew felt glad that this second act of reasonable pain had succeeded.

"Why?" Terence asked.

"Why what?"

"The light?"

"I cannot bear any more darkness," Andrew said. He drank his whisky down all in one go, but as much as he thought he needed it, he did not get up to replenish his glass.

"Then, if we must see, we must see," Terence said. His voice was a little petulant, like a sensitive child who has been reprimanded and does not know why.

"As I said, I don't like Turkey."

Andrew was insistent about getting this fact across. He had been to Istanbul once. The minarets and the markets had appalled him. Hagia Sophia. How the dreadful name suited that abominable piece of architecture. He had Christian tastes, he told himself. That place was Christian in part, but not enough. He felt most truly alive in the western part of Europe. The cathedrals of England and France were the places he liked most.

"It is so vast, Istanbul, with its two sides and its river, and that endless flow of people—like a diarrhoea that never stops."

Terence laughed at him then. "I am going there," he said.

"I didn't know we were planning a holiday."

Suddenly, even for Andrew, the light was too bright. He looked down at his empty glass, wishing it full, and listened to what Terence had to say.

"I know your prejudices," Terence said, "and knowing that made me avoid asking you to join us."

"Us?"

Andrew raised his head and they looked at each other. The single word was so urgent that it seemed to have the capacity to suck their faces together. Like a magnet, the pull of fact drew them together.

"I am going with Frederick," Terence said. "He knows that unlike you I love Istanbul, and he made it clear that it would be a boring journey for him to make alone. The other people we know all work regular hours, and he knows that I work best when I am travelling." He paused, then murmured as if to himself, "I am known for my books on travel. The one on Venice especially. You like Venice. I think you liked my book on it as well. The description of *La Fenice* especially."

Fuck *La Fenice* and all opera, Andrew thought but remained silent. His mind was shocked into harsh words, into breaking sounds. He wanted to smash the empty glass on the too perfect white of the living room's too perfect walls. But instead he gripped it between his hands, hoping if he could not throw it, that it would break in his hands and draw blood.

"Or should we have asked you, in spite of your dislike for Turkey? After all, the journey does begin in Venice and that would not have been unpleasant for you."

Andrew was slow to reply. When he did so he stared at Terence, and looked him in the eye steadily as he said, "I am one of those people who works normal hours. One of those people in our group that has a ridiculous job and gets not one jot of satisfaction from it. But when we have our dinners together, how easy it is to say that Andrew is a good lawyer and that he is the first person you should go and see when in difficulty."

Terence broke the look between them, and stared down at his empty hands, lying with pathetic helplessness in his lap. His hands needed to reach out and touch, but when Andrew looked at them he wondered to whom? To whom would they reach out and touch? Lonely as they seem, not to him.

"I am having sex with Frederick," Andrew said, the impulse to extreme cruelty now too strong to contain.

"I know," Terence replied. He moved his hands apart from each other. They fluttered for a moment in the air, odd things suddenly, ugly things, as if never before seen by man. Andrew looked at him with alien eyes.

"It is a recent thing," he continued.

"Are you in love with him?"

"I don't know. I have no heart. It is a lie inside."

"You are wrong, Andrew, about that. The heart knows when it is lying to itself. It has eyes. It sees."

"And what does your heart say?" Andrew asked mockingly.

"My heart sees that I am on a journey, that I must follow the beat of it." Terence paused before saying finally, "Then, when Frederick and I come back, all will be resumed. We will all get on with it, until of course, one or the other of us gets too tired or too bored. Maybe then we will know what meaning the word *love* has for us."

3

In the garden Frederick said, "I think it will rain tomorrow. I can smell rain the way you can smell flowers."

"You should do something about the blood," Andrew remarked at last.

Looking down at the red trickle on his arm, Frederick laughed and said that he had been caught by the thorns before, that he was used to being torn by them.

"I could get a plaster," Andrew said.

"We are not husbands, or carers, so what need is there for such a bother? My mother talks in the way you do." Then he added, "But it's only sometimes that you talk like that."

"I must sit down," Andrew said, and sat on a rockery that was nearby. Frederick was concerned and came over to him. He reached out with his bloodied arm and touched Andrew gently on the face.

"The heat of a late summer's day," he said.

"Yes, it must be that. But my heart again. It has no words, but I can almost hear it repeating that it has nowhere to go."

"You are here. Isn't that enough for it?"

"It doesn't know all about the last journey Terence made. It wants to know, Frederick. Give it at least some detail of that terminal journey. In homage to Terence who knew about the heart before I did."

"You have heard it all before," Frederick said with impatience and moved away from Andrew. He then looked up at the emptiness of the vividly blue sky, dreading the rain that he felt was coming and dreading even more the autumn that would soon be with them.

"I am going into the house," he said.

As he walked away, he let the roses that he and Andrew had gathered, drop, one by one. They were like a trail of yellow and red and faded pinks leading up the winding path to the upper garden and then on into the house. Automatically, Andrew got up and followed them, counting each one, discerning each colour. They were the tiny discarded hearts of poetry, destined to be displayed before dying, not like the real heart or the imagined heart: the heart that is held in a calculated mess of flesh and blood and that cannot be scattered at will like these blooms.

"Frederick, tell me," he said as he entered the house, the white, flimsy curtain caressing his face like a thin shroud.

"You must know. Always, again and again, you must know," Frederick said.

"Yes," Andrew replied.

Frederick paced. He was angry and he did not know why. He was repeating and repeating, and with every repetition, like a bad play being rehearsed, he got the lines wrong. But what could he say? What could he know of the exact word that even approximates to a past truth?

"We were lovers. Terence and I were lovers. It happened on the boat when we left Venice. I don't know what made the wish come true, but there on the boat it did come true."

He paused and closed his eyes. Frederick had to close his eyes so that he could enter deeper in, enter in where the heart beats at its profoundest level.

"It was not my relationship with you that killed him, but somehow his relationship with me. Maybe there were too many people on the boat who were witnesses. I cannot be sure. But I am sure that it was the love we had for each other, he and I, that killed him. Somehow it broke his heart."

Andrew reached out at the swaying white curtain to steady himself. He clutched at the fabric for a second, then let go. Inside he was falling and he allowed himself to fall. To remain sane, he thought of the beauty of the dying flowers along the path to the house, all that yellow and red and pink that would be faded and dead by the following day.

"I wanted to hear—" he began.

Frederick opened his eyes and looked at him.

"It is because of him that I dread the autumn," Frederick continued. "It was only in his arms that I felt complete. He was younger than both of us, and far more vulnerable than either you or I. I am your age and with that ten year difference I could cradle him and love him as if he were indeed that delicate child he believed he was."

"Until death came without warning," Andrew said flatly.

"Yes," Frederick replied simply. "And now you will never hear about this again. No more repetitions, ever again. If we are to remain together we must be silent about Terence. He was the best of us, but is gone."

"Now, hold my hand," Andrew said and reached out for Frederick's hand.

The clasp of fingers was strong and sure. As he reached out, Andrew thought, I hear the three of us wanting to live. The heart tells me this. It makes me faint with this knowledge, but I hear it. I must go on. Frederick will make me go on. Call it love, or any other word for that continuation.

LOVE AND PREJUDICE

It was one of those wonderful accidents. Joe and Leo were both English and living in the Netherlands but they had met one night in Rio. It was Joe's last night in Rio and as Leo had not been having much fun in the city (too much noise and too much crime) he decided to go back with Joe. The flight had apparently been full, but by another wonderful accident Leo secured a seat. They were not seated together of course (that would have been too wonderful), but at least they were on the same plane. Sitting alone in his seat (the old woman next to him was Spanish and slept most of the way) Leo marvelled at his own impetuosity. I don't know how this adventure is going to turn out, he thought, but at least for once I had the courage to act on my emotions. I never have before. He was sitting on an aisle and more often than he needed to, got up from his seat and made his way to the toilet. He had to pass Joe, who was not sitting on an aisle, but was cramped against a window, and each time he passed he would cough loudly and slow his pace. Joe, who had been told to watch for this signal, would look his way and smile that certain smile that had made Leo fall in love with him when they had met. Going back to his seat he would do the same thing: slow down and cough, but it was not necessary. Joe's smile was as wide and welcoming as the future they had both promised themselves the night before. I am a lucky man, he said to himself as he tried to make his body as comfortable as possible for sleep.

Arriving at Schiphol, Leo had a few nasty moments of panic. Somehow they got separated in the crowd and he thought he had lost Joe. They had had neither the sense nor the inclination to exchange mobile numbers or addresses, both being too preoccupied with meeting in the club and having sex in Joe's hotel afterwards. Panic overwhelmed him like a terrible black wave. At first he dashed to and fro, desperately looking. Then he imagined that Joe was probably doing the same thing, so decided it was best to remain still. He made his way to a nearby shop and stood by a gaudy rack of 400 page bestsellers. He looked out with a hopeless feeling of loss at the mass of people arriving and departing.

"Please let him come to me," he murmured aloud, and sure enough, a few seconds later, he saw Joe hurrying towards him.

"I thought I had lost you." Joe was the first to speak.

"It has been the worst time of my life," Leo replied, with all the sincere exaggeration that only those who have just fallen in love can really bring off. "I didn't know what to do, so I just prayed and stood here."

Joe laughed and had the wit to say that if he had chosen the same course of action, they would in all probability never have re-found each other.

"Let's go back to my place," Leo said.

In the taxi, they exchanged the information they had not given before. Joe lived in the heart of Amsterdam, in a small flat that he shared with a friend while Leo had a spacious apartment all to himself in the suburbs. Leo knew as he said this that the next step would be Joe moving in with him, and within a couple of weeks it happened. They had become officially a couple. A proposal of marriage might have followed, but this delightful thought had a sense of finality to it that put them both off. They also had the sense to know that the real honeymoon comes before a marriage and not after it.

"My parents should never have got married," Joe said.

Leo considered this and had to agree that it was the same with his. He remembered how his parents had constantly rowed when he was a child. He even tried to break them apart from a physical fight when he was eight.

"He was slapping her in the face, again and again," he told

Joe.

Joe looked at him and shook his head, as if dismayed at the behaviour of heterosexuals.

"Marriage is their invention, not ours," he concluded, and from that conclusion, they did not bring up the subject again.

On the whole they were happy. Joe liked the quietness of Leo's flat. It was situated in a leafy park at the end of the metro line and had all the allure of a sort of Marie Antoinette countryside existence while still being within close proximity of the city. Rabbits played in the grass, and green parrots added a touch of the exotic as they flew from tree to tree.

"It's like the Garden of Eden," Joe would say wistfully as they drank their evening cocktail on their balcony overlooking the lake.

Leo was of course pleased that the location made his lover happy, and puffed himself out like some contented and overfed pigeon. He felt pleased he had made the then dubious choice to leave central Amsterdam to come and live here.

"I was too old to carry on living in that noisy box," he said. "When the opportunity of this flat came up I jumped at the chance."

"What do you mean too old?" Joe replied.

"I am forty," Leo stated.

This was the first time he had told Joe his age. The question had somehow never come up, and he had just assumed Joe would think he was around forty anyway.

"I thought you were around thirty-two or three," Joe said.

Leo sensed a note of disappointment in Joe's voice as he said this.

"Does it matter?" Leo poured himself another cocktail while replying. If the answer was to be a disaster, then it was best if he was slightly drunk to take it. But instead of answering, Joe flashed his winning smile, and reaching across with his hand, caressed Leo's face.

"I'm very happy with you," he said at last, but looked out

at the lake instead of at Leo as he said it.

"It's just that you are so much younger than me," Leo ventured.

"Ten years. Lots of couples have an age difference."

This time he looked at Leo as he spoke, and then as if to dismiss the subject of their age difference once and for all, reminded Leo that the food already prepared inside the flat would not wait for ever.

"I have made you your favourite dish," he added with a flourish of closure.

Mornings were the only time of difficulty in their relationship. Joe took a long time in the bathroom. He was an airline steward (that was how he got a cheaper than usual flight to Rio), and he pampered himself with a lot of face creams and warm body soaking before he was ready to accept the day. Leo on the other hand was a doctor and did not feel obliged to look his best for a lot of patients who usually looked far worse than him.

"Why do you always manage to get into the bathroom before me?" he would say.

"Maybe because I am brighter in the morning than you are and get up earlier," came the smart reply.

"But you make me late for work." He did not like to reproach Joe for anything, but on this issue he had to. "I can't keep patients waiting."

Joe had no answer to this, but shrugged his shoulders as if he didn't care. This annoyed Leo more than anything.

"Can't you at least think of them?" Leo insisted.

It was a mistake to insist and Joe would go off without giving him his usual kiss. For the rest of the day, he would be miserable, and even took it out on his patients sometimes. He showed them the same lack of care that Joe had shown him. It was petty and cruel, and he knew he was behaving badly, but all the same could not control himself. One incident had been especially nasty. An older man with a Polish lover had come to the surgery. The Pole was terrified he had caught a venereal disease, and while examining him, he had been unduly brutal. His assertive probing of the youth's rectum had made him scream out with pain.

"How dare you treat him like that," the older man had said.

"I treat him in the same way I treat everybody. You should not have such an oversensitive partner."

The words had come out like a whiplash. The man looked at him in painful silence for what seemed a long time. The Pole whimpered in a corner and put on his trousers with shaking hands.

"I shouldn't have said what I said."

He mumbled the words at the man, but there was no reply. He and his lover left the surgery, and Leo lost a patient. In the evening, he told Joe what had happened.

"The man should have considered himself lucky to have an English doctor. Dutch doctors say far worse things. You know that as well as I do. From my experience, nearly all of them are insensitive."

"I have been here for twenty years. I studied here. I even took Dutch nationality."

"You are English through and through, like Brighton rock. I wouldn't be living with you if you were Dutch."

Joe smiled his wonderful smile and took Leo in his arms.

"And it is all my fault," he added. "When I work days, I take up too much time in the bathroom, but would you prefer it if I did more nights? I get out of nights as much as I can because of you."

"Thank you," Leo whispered miserably. "But say what you like, I treated that man badly."

"I expect he is used to it," Joe said, pushing Leo gently away. "He's an old man with some boy from Poland. I expect the boy is bought and paid for, and that the man gets quite a bit of stick from his friends."

"You don't know anything about him. Neither do I."

"I can imagine."

"It's wrong to imagine," Leo said angrily.

Joe laughed to break the tension. They both agreed this was leading towards a row, and they didn't want a row.

"Please don't let's ever get married."

With this retort Joe ended the conversation and their happy life took on its usual routine.

Six months after they had met, Joe got a call from England. A friend wanted to come to Amsterdam for the weekend. Joe was alone in the flat and not wanting to make a decision before Leo came back, asked his friend if he could ring him back.

"I came to live with him," he explained. "In theory it's my place too, but the fact of the matter is, the flat belongs to Leo."

His friend said that he understood.

"But I'm sure it will be alright. All I have to do is make sure with him that he has no plans for Saturday. Saturday is the one time of the week we go into Amsterdam to a club."

"Is it a good club?" the friend asked.

Joe laughed and joked about his 'bachelor days' before he met Leo. He said the club was so good, he used to go as often as he could when he wasn't flying.

"The darkroom is buzzing," he had to add.

"And I expect a lot of bees came after your special scent."

This banter went on for quite a while, and all the time, Joe felt nostalgia for a kind of conversation that he quite certainly could not have with Leo.

"Is he very Dutch?" the friend asked.

"Leo? I told you, he's English. There are absolutely no barriers between us."

The friend congratulated him on such a good find and after a few more intimate details of their life together, Joe put an end to the conversation. He then poured himself a couple of drinks, watched a porn movie and managed to relieve a few fantasies the explicit banter had provoked. Afterwards he felt slightly guilty and hid *Lost Innocence 3* at the back of his DVD collection. Soon afterwards he heard Leo come in through the door.

"I've made the drinks," he called out.

Leo did not feel good. He was very much in need of a drink. He'd had to tell a woman she had cancer. He had also had to take phone calls himself as his assistant was off sick.

"I'm not much fun this evening," he explained.

Joe did not question him. The last thing he wanted after the easy talk with his friend was to hear about a heavy day at Leo's surgery. He was also sexually excited, despite his solo performance with the DVD, and realised that this also was not going to be fun with Leo. He hated it when black moods affected their sex life.

"A friend from England called me."

They were seated facing each other. Usually they sat side by side. Joe realised that when he wanted permission for something, they often, if not always, faced each other.

"You don't often talk to your friends in England," Leo observed.

"Out of sight, out of mind," Joe said flippantly. "I guess I don't have what you'd call real friends."

"So is this friend not a real friend?"

"I've known Darren since school. He's my oldest friend. Literally. We've always known each other."

"That's good," Leo said neutrally.

Joe flashed his inevitable brightest smile and then asked if Darren could come to stay the following weekend.

"I can tell him we have other plans, but I know he'll be disappointed. It's his first time in Amsterdam."

Leo forced a laugh and replied that there always had to be a first time, and that of course Darren could come to stay.

"He's pretty easy-going," Joe added. "He'll want to do the scene, I expect. Everyone does their first time."

"It's not what it used to be," Leo said. "A long time before I stopped going to the clubs, I realised they were not what they used to be, and that other cities had got better, cleaner places."

"Yes," Joe replied, "but we English come for the myth. All hard-core."

Leo sighed and said nothing. He could see the woman's face when he had told her there was little hope. Her face had scrunched up like an old, used paper bag. Joe's talking jarred against his thoughts of this woman.

"Ring him back," he said. "Tell him it's fine by both of us."

Leo was in bed when Joe finished talking to Darren. It was past twelve, and he was anxious to get to sleep.

"I'm sorry it's so late," Joe said. "Darren's mobile was out most of the evening. Something wrong with it."

"But it's all sorted now?" Leo asked.

"Yes, he arrives at Schiphol early Friday evening. I've got time off. We can meet him together and go for a meal in Amsterdam."

Joe slid into the bed as if he was wary of Leo. There was something else that he had to tell him.

"I don't know how to say this," he began.

Leo, desperate to get to sleep, urged him to say the rest of what he had to say.

"You look worried about something, Joe. What else was he? Your lover as well as your oldest friend? If it's that, it's alright. I had lovers too, before you."

Joe laughed. It sounded hollow.

"He isn't coming alone. I'm afraid I presumed on your hospitality."

"It's your place as well as mine."

"Yes, but the person he's bringing is his boyfriend. I don't know how you feel about two of them here in the flat as well as us. Making—well, making noises."

"You mean having sex?"

Leo yawned.

"Yes."

"I don't care, Joe, as long as neither of them are kleptomaniacs. That's my only rule. Now, please, please can I get some sleep. If today, because it is already today, is anything like yesterday—" he paused and yawned again.

"I also rather wanted—"

"Me? You're horny. I should have known. I can smell it."

They both laughed at this, and Leo dutifully lay on his stomach as Joe reached for the lubricant and condoms in the bedside drawer.

Leo was the first to see Darren's boyfriend. Joe was too excited by seeing his old friend to notice, but Leo took in the situation immediately. The boyfriend was quite definitely underage, by how much he could not be certain. As Joe was about to bound forward like an excited dog, Leo held him back and said to him, "Look who he is with. He's a mere boy."

"Don't be silly," Joe replied without taking in the visual information at all and moved forward.

Darren was not, as Joe had said, exactly or even near the same age as Joe. To Leo's perceptive eye he was closer to his own age. They certainly must have been in a different class at school.

"Darren, this is Leo. Leo, this is Darren."

Leo shook hands, and then as if with one simultaneous movement, all eyes were on the boy that Darren had brought with him.

"Oh, and this is Josh," Darren exclaimed.

Josh took centre stage. He was around five foot five, thin and spotty. His long brown hair lay rather lankly over his forehead. Two rather startled eyes stared back at them. All Leo could think was, poor Josh. Then he felt angry that something was perhaps going on that he did not approve of.

"Hello," Josh said, and Leo felt a moist palm meet his own.

"Is this your first time in Amsterdam as well?" Leo asked, in the tone of voice of a person talking to a child.

"Yes," came the small-voiced reply.

"He's been wanting to see Amsterdam for so long," Darren added. His voice was rather high pitched and squeaky, and Leo immediately thought that he didn't like the sound or the look of the man.

"We've come by car," Joe said. "Leo's car. We can take a walk in Amsterdam first before going back to the flat to eat. Alternatively, we could have something to eat in the city."

"I live in the suburbs," Leo said rather ominously.

"Tomorrow, I'd like to go on a canal ride."

Josh had found his voice and aired an objective. He smiled at Leo as he said this, and the way he looked was rather pleading, as if to say, please don't be an enemy. I have enough trouble as it is.

No one replied to him and all four hurried out of the airport. Once in the car, everyone was silent, thinking separate and no doubt very private thoughts.

The evening in Amsterdam was approached with a maximum amount of politeness. Leo was the most polite, pointing out various places of interest and commenting on points of history. Darren looked disinterested, but Josh listened to every word Leo said, and added a few comments of his own.

"I especially want to see the tower where they set out for America," he said.

Leo made them all wander over to the said tower, then taking them down a nearby canal, pointed out an inexpensive Chinese restaurant.

"I love Chinese food," Josh said.

"It makes me ill," Darren muttered, then added that this was not always true and that he would go along with the rest. The meal however proved to be a disaster, both in culinary terms and as far as conversation was concerned. Joe could see that Leo was quietly furious, and from time to time he looked over at Darren, hoping to relay by eye contact that all was not well. But Darren had his eyes fixed on his plate, as he picked at shrimp and noodle with vague disgust.

Then the bomb exploded. It was Leo who lit the fuse.

"How old are you?" he asked Josh.

Josh looked at Leo as if he was a policeman who had suddenly entered the bedroom.

"Eighteen," he said.

"How old are you?" Leo repeated.

Darren threw down the chopsticks he was uselessly using and said, "Well, really!"

Josh was in a panic. He looked first at Darren, then at Joe who had both looked away. It was as if he was alone with Leo, and a question he did not want to answer truthfully.

"How old?" Leo repeated again, but more gently.

"Fourteen," came the quiet reply.

"I can explain," Darren interrupted, but Leo waved a hand at him as if brushing away a rather unpleasant mosquito.

"I don't think you can," he said.

Joe managed to put in a word of defence.

"It really isn't any of our business."

Leo turned to Joe.

"When is it not my business when a fourteen year old boy is passed off as being eighteen? When he has no doubt been told to pass himself off as eighteen? I think it is very much my business. Especially when this boy is going to end up in my apartment, in my spare room, in the same bed as a man old enough, at the very least, to be his father."

"Do you have to be so crude?"

Darren glared at Leo across the table.

"Yes," Leo replied. "I am English enough to want to remain silent and Dutch enough to want to be direct."

"Pompous is more like it," Joe said with a surge of contempt.

At that moment the whole thing fell apart. The room might

as well have been blown to bits. If there were no corpses there was certainly very little left to salvage. Leo turned to Joe and murmured quietly to him, "It is all over. I suppose you know that."

"And to think I thought you were more open in your approach to things. But then I suppose there were always signs that you had a narrow mind. A Dutch mind."

"Call it what you like Joe," Leo said, "but Darren and Josh cannot stay in the apartment."

"Your apartment," Joe spat out, accentuating the *your*.

"Whatever you want to call it," Leo said wearily. He had caused the destruction, but now all he wanted was to get up and leave. Only a sense of pity for the boy made him stay at the table. He looked over at Darren who had remained silent.

"I know nothing about you," Leo said, "but I have a feeling you can only cause Josh harm."

"He's fine to me," Josh interrupted. His voice was shaking and his eyes were filled with unspilled tears.

"Yes, that's what you think now," Leo gently replied, "but later?"

"You are such a fucking moralist." Joe was now bitingly furious. "A fucking moralist who has absorbed all this Calvinist double-think. The Dutch hate everything that isn't normal. They hate homosexuals. They have a history of double standards. Boy bars, S & M, the lot have been allowed, still are, but less so, yet all the time, hated by the people who tolerate it. A crazy, fucked-up people, and you have taken on their nationality."

Leo got up then. He struck Joe in the face and walked out of the restaurant. Sobbing as he walked, he made his way down the canal to where he had parked his car.

Joe came once to pack his things. He ignored Leo and Leo could not open a conversation. When he had finished packing, he threw the keys to the flat onto the table.

"Where are you going?"

The words came out with difficulty, as if Leo was trying to talk through the horror of strangulation. But Joe continued to ignore him, and Leo, with a hollow feeling of emptiness, realised he would never again have Joe taking up too much time in the bathroom. He closed his eyes and heard the outer door slam. As if in a nightmare, he heard the too loud music of the Rio club, and put his hands to his ears in a futile attempt to shut out an inner and frighteningly persistent sound.

COWARDICE

Que voulez-vous de plus
Que voulez-vous de moi

(What more do you want
What do you want of me)

- Jacques Prévert -

Everyone of a certain age who was involved in it has their personal memories of May 1968 in Paris. I use the word *involved* advisedly, because so many of us were bystanders, watching the man-made barricades against the police from a distance, often after the fight was over, after the demonstration was ended. I admit to being one of those people. I was too busy, in the heart of Saint-Germain-des-Prés, having fun in a basement club primarily for homosexuals called *La Boîte à Chansons*. From there, while we danced and called out to each other, the sound of revolt could be heard on the boulevard. As the sounds grew louder we shrieked louder, mockingly clinging to our temporary partners as if we were afraid of being disturbed, afraid of being hurt in the battle. Then one night there was the faint smell of tear gas, and we heard cries and the running of feet outside of the club door. At first we took no notice of it, and one of our regulars, a tall blond boy, began to dance. We switched our attention from the street to him, watching as he danced around the small space of floor, shouting out a song from the Astaire and Rogers film *Follow the Fleet* which was

149

currently being re-run in a small cinema in the rue Champollion. He spoke rather than sang out the words from *Let's Face the Music and Dance*, and we lined the walls clapping and applauding him, making music with our hands to accompany the words. I stood very close to him, as usual entranced by the beauty of his body and the rhythmic patterns it could make. For so many months I had desired him, but as yet I had not been chosen to be his companion for a night. Then when he had reached the end of the song, he stopped, but the crowd was almost feverish with excitement at the sight of him, shirt unbuttoned to the waist, and urged him to continue, to repeat the song.

"I am tired," he shouted, but still the others persisted.

He took off his shirt and I was the one to catch it when he threw it from him. It was wet with perspiration, and as he returned to making his own pattern to the words we all sang out the lyrics for him.

"Cowards!"

The voice rang loud and clear, rising above our own. I turned to where the sound came from and saw a youth standing at the bottom of the stone stairs which led up to the club entrance. He had blood on his face and his black hair was half red from it.

"Cowards!" he repeated.

We stared at him, most of us shocked into silence. Reality had broken its way into our world, and stood unsteadily before us. He was handsome, most of us could see that, and this aspect of his being had an equal fascination for us along with the blood and the echoes of violence he had brought with him. He opened his mouth again, but only stared at us from this shallow distance, unable to repeat again what he had said or to add further words.

"He is ill."

"No, he just has a surface wound to his head."

"Jean-Paul, we must do something."

The chorus of speculation about his condition spread

among us like a forest fire. We were caught up in his appearance of wounding or illness, and being strangers to the sight of it, none of us appeared to want to go to him. It was only when he lurched forwards, as if to break into the cube of our dance floor that I made a simultaneous movement and went towards him.

"I need water," he said as I reached him, staring at me with a mixture of anger, fear and an instinctive need to be helped.

"Simone," I called out to one of the people working there that night, "please bring him some water from the bar."

The others, still fixed in their standing position, watched with curiosity as the woman detached herself from the crowd and went behind the bar to get him a drink. She was quick and handed it to me, not wanting to hand it to him herself.

"What side is he on?" she asked me as I took the glass from her hand.

"What side do you think?" I replied coldly, then turning to the boy who looked as if he was about to pass out, placed the glass in his hand and helped him raise it to his lips. He drank the water down in one go.

The crowd behind me, sensing the situation in front of them was losing its dramatic power, began to move around, and the DJ hurriedly put on some Nicoletta. A few shuffled onto the dance floor and I guided the youth away from them into one of the furthest recesses of the club. I found a wide plush chair, a reproduction antique in the style of Louis XV, and sat him down on it. He stared up at me in silence, then handed the glass back to me.

"Rest," I said.

"I don't want to be among these men," he replied, then reached up and touched the place where he had been wounded.

"I want to see how bad it is," I said, then reaching out I parted his thickly curled black hair and saw that the skin had been nastily, though superficially, broken open.

"Simone," I called again.

She came over to me, a little impatient that I had taken this intruder to one of the most private places of the small club. This was where she or the other person who ran the place sat and watched out for their customers' welfare. I could see by the expression on her face that she was worried he would get blood all over the chair.

"Is it bad?" she asked.

"No, I just need a small bowl. I know you have one in case someone gets sick. Can you find it and fill it with warm water and also find a clean cloth so I can wipe the wound? Oh, and yes, a plaster and some bandages from the emergency box."

"Anything else?" she asked sarcastically.

The youth moved restlessly in the chair, then made an attempt to get up, but fell back, no doubt giddy with the effort.

"I'm okay now," he said and closed his eyes.

Simone moved away and I called after her to bring a couple of aspirin from the emergency box as well. As I was a regular at the bar, she obeyed me, but I could tell that the next time I came to the place she would reprimand me for not having flung him back onto the street. She was conservative and a fervent supporter of De Gaulle, and I realised with a sense of sadness the she was not alone in the club with these convictions. The youth in front of her was just a bloody (literally) troublemaker, out to make a fuss and unbalance the normal course of power. She knew quite definitely what side she was on. After all, she was older than the rest of us and had seen what De Gaulle had done for France at the end of the war.

"I want to get out of here," the youth said.

I told him to be patient and after a short while, Simone returned with all the things I had asked for.

It took me a few minutes to wipe his wound clean, and then with a rapidity that amazed even me, I covered it with a plaster, turned to get another drink and forced the aspirins down his throat. He smiled at me, and the smile was open and genuinely thankful.

"Why aren't you out there?" he asked. "Why are you in here with this bunch of clowns?"

"Maybe because I too am one of the clowns, as you call us."

"What's your name?"

"Julian. With an A. The English way. I am English."

"Olivier."

"I'd like to say, nice to meet you Olivier, but perhaps this is not what you want to hear."

"Is this a place for—" he actually said the word *pédés*, but followed it swiftly with a slight alteration, "Is this a place for them?"

"It is for anyone with an open mind," I said.

He laughed at this, and raised his hand to the plaster and the extra bandage that I had also wound about his head.

"Well, I seem to have a sort of open head," he joked feebly. Then he got up and smiling at me made his way towards the entrance. The blond boy who had been dancing, came up to him and shouted, "Are you going so soon? It seems a pity to lose a misguided revolutionary so quickly."

I went to the blond who was called Laurent and told him to clear off. He sneered at me, baring his beautifully white 16^e arrondissement teeth and replied, "Well, my friend, that's a quick pick-up, even for here."

"Let's go," I said to Olivier who clearly wished he had the strength to punch Laurent. "He's not worth it," I added, as if reading his thoughts. "Save your strength for the other fight."

We made our way up the steps to the outside door, then found ourselves on the narrow street. We were only a few paces from the boulevard St-Germain, and I guided Olivier away from it, urging him gently with my hand on his arm in the direction of the Seine.

"I don't live in this direction," he murmured.

I noticed he was still unsteady on his feet and asked him how far away he lived from where we were.

"I have a *chambre de bonne* off the rue d'Alésia," he said.

"You're not well enough to go that distance," I replied. "You can barely walk, you are so done in. I live nearby. You can stay with me until morning. I promise I won't touch you."

Again the bright sound of his laughter.

"You wouldn't get much out of me," he said, "not in this state. God, I really do feel as if I'm going to pass out. There's still a lot of gas in the air. I can hardly breathe."

"Then come back with me."

I lived in one of the narrow streets off the boulevard St-Michel. Surprisingly there was no-one much on the streets, despite the fact that it had all been a war zone. We passed an overturned car, all burnt out.

"I did that," he said jokingly, "with my own special brand of Molotov cocktail." Then he added slyly, "Not the sort of cocktails you drink at the dump I fell into."

"How did you fall in?" I asked.

"Got pushed by a good friend who said I would be safe there. He had been hit harder than I was, but still he put me first."

"Why didn't he come in with you?"

"He has a girl. Despite how badly he was hit, he said he had to find her."

"Is he a student as well?"

"A student? We are workers. In a factory. But we have thought and we have read and we have taken action."

We reached the house: a narrow medieval looking building that pointed itself way upwards into the dark sky.

"There's lots of stairs," I said.

"I'll take them one at a time," he replied, and we entered the house.

My small flat was on the top floor. There was a blackened wall facing the only windows that I had, and of course, no view. By day, it was only a shade lighter than at night. No sunlight ever came in.

"You've got two rooms," he said. "You must be *un fils à papa.*"

"He's in England. He's not rich, and he certainly does not pay for this. I have a job at the Sorbonne teaching English. I also work at a bar near Saint-Sulpice several evenings a week to pay for extras like eating."

He looked at me for the first time with a degree of admiration, and asked me if I had ever joined the *others* who were protesting.

"No," I replied honestly.

"Why?"

"Look, you are tired. Lie down on that sofa for fuck's sake and close your eyes for a while."

He looked at the sofa, then shook off his shoes and lay down on it. But his eyes, which were dark brown, still watched my every movement. I pretended not to notice and going into the kitchen area, which was in the corner of the room, made him some food. I too was hungry and I made two large pâté baguettes. All the time I had my back to him I could feel his gaze, and for a moment I had the absurd expectation that he would come over to me and put his arms around me. Shrugging off the thought as stupid but natural enough for me, I returned to the sofa and gave him the food. He took it, but while I ate with appetite, he nibbled at the bread. I sensed he still felt too unwell to take in food.

"Why are you homosexual?" he asked suddenly.

"I am what I am," I replied, quite consciously quoting from Prévert. But I am not sure he noticed the literary reference. "And you are, no doubt, what you are," I added.

"Yes," he said, then placed the plate with the baguette on the floor by the sofa. I was sitting near him on the chair by my desk. It was in this room, most nights, very late, that I corrected my students' essays. It was here at this desk that I confronted their confusions with the English language.

"I had a girl until recently," Olivier said. His voice was quiet, and lying out, full length on the sofa, he placed a hand on his covered wound.

"The aspirins must be wearing off," I said. "I have more here. I think you should take a couple to keep the pain at bay."

"You're being very kind," he replied. The words were said sincerely without a trace of sarcasm.

"Not at all. Someone had to help you."

"But you did," he replied. Then after a moment's cautionary silence, he asked me if I found him attractive. He said that he wanted to know, and the way in which he asked, with such simplicity, made me want to reply truthfully.

"If you had gone to that bar in the same way as the others, then yes I would have found you attractive, and yes, if you had reciprocated that attraction, we would in all probability be in the same place we are now. But that's not how it was, is it?"

"No," he said.

"But Olivier, please don't get me wrong. I find a lot of young men attractive and there is no reason for you to feel threatened here. I never attempt anything with heterosexual boys."

"I like you," he half whispered, then pulled himself into a sitting position and stared around at the room. "You have a lot of books. I read a lot as well. Mostly political, but I have a love of poetry. I see you have Rimbaud. His image is now all over the rooms and streets of Paris. He is like us: against conformity."

I smiled as he said this, then looking down at the floor, as if for some strange reason I dared not face him, replied, "He also had a male lover. He may now be one of *yours*, as you put it, but he is one of *ours* as well. He was homosexual for quite a while in his youth. With Verlaine. You must know that."

I raised my head to look for a reaction on Olivier's face. I knew that there were still many people in France who were in denial about Rimbaud's sexuality. At the best they thought of his same-sex activities as being forced on him by the nasty sodomite Verlaine. Rimbaud, in the homosexual sense, was a victim of abuse, not a chooser of his desires, or of Verlaine.

"I don't know much about all that," he said at last. "For me he is a symbol of a sort of anarchic freedom that so many of us now desire. That is all. And that kind of freedom is not just a privilege for students. And anyway his poems don't mention his sex with another man."

"It was more forbidden in his times than even now," I parried. "And anyway, it is there, between the lines."

"I don't read between the lines."

He got up and walked around the room. He stopped at the bookcase and picked out a few books here and there as if he had every intention of taking them away and reading them. He seemed to single out a work on Trotsky that an acquaintance had given me. I told him he was free to take it away.

"Don't you want it?" he asked.

"No. It's not really my battle, the one you are fighting. A woman friend gave it to me last Christmas. She's a communist."

"And what are you?"

I replied that I had no particular convictions. Only the conviction of being an outsider.

"But we are all outsiders," he replied.

"Then I am outside your sense of the outside."

The words were clumsy, but he understood them.

"Does your desire for men get in the way of being involved?" he asked.

The question was astute and in its direct way true. The fight for freedoms on the Paris barricades was no place it seemed for people like me. As homosexuals, we were somehow lumped in with the other bourgeois rubbish that they wanted to clear away.

"I don't think you care that men like me, or women like me, are oppressed as well," I said.

He looked at me and his face looked weary. He shook his

head and could only say that he had never thought about it seriously. He added that most of the men he saw who were homosexual looked far too comfortable, far too out of reach in their way of life in society, and finally, far too conservative.

"It's a defence mechanism," I said.

It was at that moment that he did the strangest thing. He came up to me and kissed me on the lips. He forced my mouth open and I felt his tongue probing my mouth. It felt exploratory and without passion. It felt as if it were searching for knowledge that for some reason was necessary for him. It was a kiss that he needed himself to understand. After he had finished, for despite my attraction to him I did not reciprocate, he broke from me and then covered his mouth as if he wanted to wipe away what he had done.

"Olivier."

I just said his name, and at the sound of it, he rushed to the bookcase and picking up the volume of Rimbaud's poems, threw it violently onto the floor.

"Damn him," he said, then returned to the sofa where he sat hunched on the edge.

At that point I left him to himself. I went into the bedroom and lay down on the bed. I stayed like that for a long time in semi-darkness. I had left the door slightly open and I could hear him moving around. I would be lying to say that I didn't feel afraid, because I did. He had wanted to fulfil some need, some knowledge that he needed to know and it was not for me to question the mystery of it. But I feared violence against myself, and also the violence that I could possibly inflict on him.

"Julian."

I heard him call my name. I got up and went back into the room. He was standing by the door. He smiled at me as if nothing had happened, then murmured the words, "I must thank you. For everything you did for me tonight. If I have abused you in any way, I am sorry. As for the Rimbaud—"

He paused, and I said, "Fuck sodding Rimbaud."

He laughed then: a fresh laugh, and the look on his face said that he was ready for a new day, for a new battle.

"I thought you were a coward not to be out there with us," he said, "but now I don't think you are. How wonderful the meaning of the kiss must be for you. The kiss between men that we on the so-called barricades are too cowardly ourselves to understand. How wonderful and fulfilling when it is truly, deeply felt. For a moment I wondered about myself. I wondered about that frontier of another sort of freedom that I had never really thought of before, or respected. I thought this while I kissed you, but there was no desire other than thought. I loved you as a brother then, and one day—yes, one day, I will join you on your barricades. I will be there for you in brotherhood when the time comes."

"It may never come," I replied.

"One day it will. A kiss is too great a thing to not fight for." He opened the door, and said, "You also came to me when no one else did. You treated me as an equal. That was certainly no act of cowardice."

Then he disappeared out of my life. I heard his steps descend the stairs, and as I closed my door I stared at the dark wall outside of my windows. It was becoming lighter outside. I hoped another, perhaps better day, was beginning.

For no reason that I can recall I reached up with my fingers and touched my lips.

A DAY OF PERFECT HAPPINESS

She is tired. She sits on a bench in the square. She looks at the rundown Regency houses, and glances quickly to the bottom of the road. She never walks down to where the once complete and once beautiful West Pier used to be. She has no desire to look at the empty ruins of it that remain in the sea. Decades ago she used to be driven down by her then Italian lover and somehow he would always manage to get a room with a perfect view of the pier at the Hotel Metropole with its endless red carpeted corridors and its sharp snobbish smell of 1950s luxury. He would sit by the open window, a green penguin detective book at hand, occasionally picking it up, reading a page or two, drinking a little whisky and then staring out at the sight of the West Pier and the promenade he loved so much. Was it because of him she had chosen to make Brighton the last place she would live? She brushed the thought aside as if it was an annoying fly. Piero had been her lover, but she had not been in love with him. In fact she was quite bored with him most of the time. Bored with his lawyer job and his underhand tricks to get more money from his clients. Bored with the way he would listlessly lie around all day in his expensive Kensington apartment, reading his dreary murder mysteries and occasionally making love to her. She remembers how she went through the motions of love-making with him, always holding back, giving a semblance of passion to keep him satisfied. Why? Why had she chosen such a wrong man? Why had she endured the boredom of his company? Her life was fresh with grief then and she knows she chose him because he was the first to come along.

Brighton in the fifties. She sighs as she sits on the bench. Regency Square had its faded elegance then, but it was gentler, kinder. The houses were not so marked or ill-used with age and neither were there hideous skyscrapers overshadowing it. She could never have imagined she would end up in the 1990s in a shabby room in the square: a corridor of a room, only big enough for a long, thin bed, a side table and a chair. She moves a little restlessly on the bench. She is so thin and she gets uncomfortable quickly, and there is this cough that will not go away. She knows she has a fever but she has no thermometer in her room and refuses to see a doctor. Her mind wanders back, back to the days when she had raced down to Brighton in Piero's sports car. The journey had always invigorated her. She needed constant motion then, constant movement, to forget. During that brief London to Brighton journey she had the intoxication of speed. Once in the hotel, while Piero was reading and looking out of the window she would make some excuse about needing something at the shops. She would leave him for a couple of hours and wander along the promenade, and yes, go onto the West Pier, have tea there and look back at the red façade of the Metropole, gaily flying flags and always looking its superior self. So long ago. She sighs again, then coughs violently. For a while she has trouble breathing. She catches at her throat with her hand, as if to prevent a strangling. Her mind races faster than any sports car. Piero. Yes, him. The man she had met after the death of her husband. She was in her thirties then, and now she is in her seventies. I never thought I would live so long, she thinks and the breathing suddenly becomes easier. Why did I come to Brighton to live? She tries to forget she is ill by asking herself questions that are easy to face, easy to acknowledge, unlike the death of her husband. But no, she must not go there. Not yet. Not just now. Save it for the last. Concentrate on the *why* of coming to Brighton. It has been ten years that I have lived here, she says. Is she talking aloud? She looks quickly around her, but no one is interested, no one is noticing. She remembers that in her sixties, she could no longer bear the pace of London, not even

Bloomsbury where she had had a more comfortable room. The fast pace of London had been too much for her and so she had chosen Brighton. Her mother had lived here after her father had died and so had her sister and her brother. All dead. All gone. She shudders. She is the last, and this is the last of days. She cannot call this city home. It is in no way home. Home died when her husband died. The coughing starts up again and she cuts off that train of thought. She looks down with her bad eyes at the white raincoat she is wearing. It is as fragile as herself, but can easily be washed out at night and hung up in her room. It's a hot summer's day, and she senses she is slightly ridiculous wearing a raincoat when there is absolutely no forecast for rain. But then, she has no other coat, except her winter coat. She has that, two pairs of shoes and a couple of dresses and blouses. She has only what she can carry around in one suitcase. It has been like that since she walked out on Piero in the 1960s when she at last made the decision to face life on her own, to live in one room, with her one suitcase and her portable radio. She smiles. It is suddenly comforting to have so few comforts.

"I have lived in rented rooms since his death."

She is sure she has said this aloud. She really must be careful. What else might she say aloud in public without realising it? But she is not going mad. No, she is in no danger of that. She has a fever. That is why she is not always sure about what she is doing. She puts her hand into her raincoat pocket and brings out a pair of sunglasses. Her eyes are tired, and she can close them without people seeing that she has closed them. She feels protected by them when she wants to close her eyes in public. One room. Only one room. Her thoughts are wandering and her body violently shudders. A spasm. It soon passes. At first she thinks she is going to pitch forward off the bench, but the frightening sensation passes. She knows she is possibly seriously ill, but she no longer cares. She wants it all to end. Then she is conscious that a woman has sat down beside her.

"Lovely day."

She does not reply to the comment.

"I said it's a lovely day."

How long can she keep up the silence? How long before she has to say something, to assume the responsibility of dialogue? That, or to get up suddenly and move away. She tries to raise herself up, but her body feels like lead. She seems to be chained to the bench.

"It's a lovely day to take a walk along the promenade."

It seems the woman will not give up until she replies, so she takes off her sunglasses and looks at the person sitting next to her. She notices at once that she is around the same age as herself.

"Yes. It is lovely."

She forms the polite words with her polite accent, acquired at Roedean. She is still proud of the fact that she had an education at Roedean. Impulsively she wants to tell the woman this. The woman has a common accent. She is proud that she doesn't have a common accent. None of her family ever spoke with a common accent. I am a snob, she thinks, and then smiles at what the world of 1998 would call an unpleasant thought.

"I like to sit here on a sunny day," the woman resumes. "I don't like to sit in them tired old shelters. The glass is always broken, and then there's the danger. You can be got at so much more easily in one of them shelters than you can on this bench."

She smiles at the woman saying, "I don't sit here very often."

"What's your name, love?"

"Vanessa," she says and has a vivid memory of her father calling her Nessa and how one day over lunch she had cheekily asked for fifty pounds and he had immediately given it to her. Her mother had glared at her impudence, and her brother had pushed away his chair and sulkily left the table without having a dessert. She had been her father's favourite child and she had abused his love in so many small ways. But none so shocking as asking him for fifty pounds over a Sunday lunch. She had been twenty then.

"What's it for?" her mother had asked.

"She doesn't have to tell me that," her father had replied.

"Too much love," her mother had said; her mother who had never had too much love from her father.

"He gave me fifty pounds," she says aloud to the woman. "It was a lot then."

"When dear?"

"I am sorry. I am thinking aloud. How rude of me."

The woman's laugh is as bright as the sunlight. Vanessa wants to put on her sunglasses again, but knows that too would be rude.

"I am always talking to myself," the woman says. "It's a habit that comes with—you know what."

She didn't know what. She stares blankly at the woman.

"Age, love. You know. Old."

"Oh, yes."

She turns away from the woman and rubs at a spot of dirt on her raincoat.

"I'm Debbie," the woman says. "Like Debbie Reynolds."

"Yes. How nice."

Vanessa holds out her own, brown-spotted hand. Her own old hand. Debbie shakes it in surprise. She is clearly not used to shaking people's hands. The action creates awkwardness. Time for both women to get up and walk away. Neither do.

"You've got a lovely name," Debbie insists.

"Thank you," she replies quietly.

Reluctantly she turns round to face the woman who calls herself Debbie. She was brought up to be polite in all social situations, and this may be one of her last. So she must do her best before she can escape from the bench.

"Do you live in Brighton?" Debbie asks.

"Yes."

"For long?"

"Ten years."

"I suppose you and your other half moved here then."

A wave of shock as she hears the expression *other half*. It was severed, severed so brutally, long, long ago. Back in the late forties. She pushes the impending, crowding images aside. No, not now. Time enough to think of all that later.

"I am alone," she says quite simply.

"Oh dear. We are a pair. So am I." Debbie laughs a long, brittle laugh. It is so loud, it makes the waves of light dance. "My husband had a fatal stroke and it isn't funny at all, but there he was in the middle of a four letter word when he had it. It was all over very quickly. But what an awful word he chose to die on."

She's not used to coarseness any more. Of course she knows all the four letter words. During the war she had been an ambulance driver. She had even been friends with a famous actress of the day who managed to get her a job as an extra in a film. She had heard every bad word then, and details of sexual activities (especially among the men) which she didn't understand or approve of. Oh yes, she had been around, but she had always hated it when things became coarse. That film director who had hired her—what was his name? A friend of Noel Coward and that lot. He had often sworn at her actress friend.

"I hope I haven't shocked you. You've gone awful silent."

If Roedean had taught her anything it was manners. She must use them now. It's as if suddenly she is young again and being very, very social.

"No, I am just being silly. I've been rather ill recently. Flu. But over it now. Over it completely."

"Flu's nasty," Debbie says. "I've had my jab, so I'm immune. Oh, I wouldn't go a year without my jab."

Slight pause.

"D'you have one, dear?"

"What?"

"A jab?"

She hates doctors. The doctors did nothing to save her husband. Maybe they thought he deserved to die. How dare this woman bring up the thought of doctors.

"No," she replies simply.

"Not this year, or never?"

"Not this year."

It is simple to lie. How wonderful it would be to be capable of lying to oneself, but that is an art she has never perfected. Always, always she has been aware of the ravages and the losses. Only sometimes when the radio played music from the late thirties or forties did she manage to forget the haunting truths. All those wonderful songs she had loved so much when she was a girl and a young woman. The songs she had listened to with her actress friend and the dances she had danced before she had met—she must stop right now. How could she be sure she would not be foolish enough to tell this woman all about it? In her fever, to tell her the truth? To tell her his name? Impossible.

"I really must be going soon."

She says this in her politest voice. She opens her tired eyes as wide as possible and stares hard at Debbie. How loudly the woman dresses. She could not deny that they were expensive clothes, but so cheap to look at. Gaudy somehow. The colours clashing in the summer light. As loud and vibrant in their ugliness as the woman's voice. Silver earrings dangling from her ears, not matching at all her dyed bluish hair. Rings glistening, practically all over her fingers.

"It must be late. It's silly, but I have left my watch at home."

Debbie looks at her watch.

"Oh, I've got plenty of time, dear. The pictures don't start for another two hours. Had a late lunch, so I don't need to eat."

Another short pause.

"Look, why don't you come to the pictures with me? I know they don't make them like they used to, but if you choose right you can get a passable old-fashioned romance."

She shrinks at the thought of it. The last picture, as the woman calls it, that she had seen was *English Without Tears* and she cannot even begin to remember how long ago that was.

"It's so kind of you to ask me, but the flu has made me so weak. I really must go soon and rest."

"Maybe I can walk you back to your place."

Not to my room she thinks. I will face that alone, as I have faced so much alone for so long. Nothing to make me afraid there. Or is there?

"I will be alright, and it's so kind—"

Debbie stops her.

"Why kind? I'm just a bit concerned about you."

"You don't know me," she says. For a moment the politeness has gone from her voice. The words almost sound like an accusation.

"I'm just trying to be friendly."

Then it hits her. The panic hits her. She cannot stand the irritating way people will interfere, trying to make changes, to change her course. Her course in life has gone too far. It cannot be altered at the very end, and here she is at the very end.

"I don't want help!"

She cries out rudely. She cries out as she cried out at Roedean one day when they made her play games she didn't want to play; shouts out as she shouted out at her mother after her husband's death. All her life, people getting close, when the only person who really got close to her had his life cut short.

"I don't need anyone to be concerned."

Her voice is hard as gravel. She can hear it. It is the same voice she used in a temper with her younger sister. She had been reaching for a clothes hanger at the time, and catching at it, had whisked it off the rail and the metal hook had slashed across her sister's face.

"I am completely alone. Just leave me completely alone."

She lowers her head, ashamed of her anger. It comes like this. This brutal, unremitting anger. It lashes out at anyone who dares to reach too far. When she raises her head, she sees that the woman has gone. The woman called Debbie has left her, as she said she wanted to be, alone.

"No one knows me now," she says aloud. "No one has the right to know me now."

Inside, her Roedean friendships, her actress friend's love, and her father's love, all go down in the flood. She is drowning.

"I must—"

What must she?

"I must."

The sentence ends. She must do nothing, nothing but wait. Pause here on this bench as the sun begins to go down in the sky. Wait as the people drift away along the promenade, leaving empty spaces in which to glance at the distant sea. To look at the tawdry remnants of what was once intense colour and the vivid flow of life on the pier. This is Brighton now, and the day is passing, as all desire to resist the last desire for life is passing. She must only wait for the minimum of energy to return so that she can go back to her room.

"Easy now."

She raises herself up. A group of youths brush against her, almost pushing her back down upon the wood.

"I must be very easy now with myself."

At last she finishes the sentence properly about what she must do. In her youth, her mother had always reprimanded her for not finishing her sentences.

"How can people know what you mean?"

She shrugs as she straightens up. She is on her feet. The chains of the bench have fallen away. All she has to do now is to put one foot in front of the other and turn her body towards the street. She lives in a room at the top of the square, in the right hand corner as you go up from the sea. It is in a house near to a pub where she and Piero drank; those few times when he was willing to leave the whisky in the room and go out with her. Piero. She shrugs again. He too gone. Died fifteen years ago while she was still in London. She had gone to the funeral, but few of the people there knew who she was or cared.

She struggles up the street. Once or twice she has to grasp at a railing. This weakness is getting stronger and she cannot, cannot collapse in the street. She cannot die in the street like some animal.

"It cannot be the end just yet, and certainly not before I have looked at the photo one last time."

She does not mind speaking these words aloud. They are keeping her going. The sound of her own voice is keeping her going. It is the only sound now left in the vacant space that has become her life.

"I want to see the photo."

She says it louder, over and over again. A couple pass her, and she is conscious that they are staring at her. Only a few more houses to go, then turn the corner and she will cease to be a public attraction.

"Benny."

At last she says his name. Benny, short for Benito. Italian, but he had changed it to Benny. After all, hadn't he the same name as Mussolini, and England wasn't the place, then in the forties, to have a name like that.

"Benny."

She says it again. It gets her to the corner, and she turns into the last stretch towards the house where she lives. She does not ask aloud, but she wonders if that had not been the sole reason, the only reason why she had chosen Piero: another Italian, to remind and not to remind her of her dead husband. Piero had been her punishment for all the wrong she had inflicted upon her devoted and loving, but weak, husband.

"I must remember now," she says aloud. "I must remember now before it all goes."

She reaches the house. The paint is peeling off the walls, but the house used to be charming. She turns the key in the lock, and walks unsteadily inside. It is very old and musty. She looks around her, wary in case she meets anyone else who lives there. She doesn't want to meet her neighbours who are all solitary people, and all old. Up the stairs. One at a time. What bad luck to have the small corridor of a room at the top of the house. Then the key, the second and last key on her ring to let her into the barren room. It is so quiet. The silence thunders in her head.

"I would normally put on the radio," she says, "but not tonight."

She sits on the edge of the bed. She looks around the room. Yes, she is sad. She admits to herself that she is sad. She really does not want to die in this room. But the money her rich husband left her in trust is almost depleted and this is all she can afford.

"It is fortunate the money was eked out to get me this far."

The words make her momentarily panic. This is the final part of life. She is in her final room and she is facing it, and there is neither the willpower to live, nor money left in the bank to keep her alive. The cough attacks again. Savage this time. Pain as well. Equally savage.

"Vanessa."

She calls her own name. She needs a friend.

"Vanessa, what are you to do?"

She gets up off the bed with immense difficulty. She is unsteady and feels drunk with the pain in her chest. She crosses to the wardrobe, and reaching up to the top-most shelf, catches at a box. It almost falls on top of her grey hair, but she manages to contain it in her frail hands. She returns to the bed and lies out full-length upon it.

"Benny."

She repeats his name again. She opens the box and there among letters and scraps left from decades past, picks out one photo: the only photo that she has of him. They are sitting by a lake. Lake Como. It is a fine day, very much like today with the sun shining. The sun is bright, shining through the darkness of the black and white photo. He is staring out at the camera (Who was taking the photo? Gone. Gone too. Cannot remember.), while she is staring at him. She can see even with her now very tired eyes, the lively smile that is playing on her lips as she looks at him. Oh, how much she had loved him then. A day of perfect happiness. Then the pain in her chest kicks in badly, and she cries out. Mentally, she is in a room and she is waving a phone in her hands, and she is crying out, "He is dead, he is dead, he is dead." Nothing and no one can calm her. And what had happened? An overdose of aspirins. Taken in despair because he hated London, because he was tired of life and tired of being the victim of a war he had never approved of. Because of the pain in his mind he had taken the whole bottle of pills, and she had been the one to find him dying in the bathroom. Then the hospital and the stomach pump, and the false words of the doctor that he would be alright, that he would recover. She had been told to go home, to get some rest as the hospital was full and there was no bed vacant for an Italian suicide's wife. She had got back to the house where her mother was waiting for her and even before the key turned in the lock she heard the phone ringing.

"He is dead, he is dead, he is dead."

Then the reaching out of oblivion, as it was reaching out now. She lay back on the bed and tried to focus her eyes on this recorded happy day, taken by who knows who. Benny had loved her and he had come to live in London for her. But he was a stranger there, whose father had been a rich industrialist. He had no one in London but her, and he had clung to her too fiercely, and she had been angry and frustrated at his hunger and his need.

"Why don't you go out and get a job like everyone else?"

She had screamed at him one day. She had shouted at him that he was a good for nothing, lazy Italian and that he was weak. He was weak because he was too kind and loving.

"I love you," he had said, and she had shut herself away from him in the bedroom. Many hours later, she found him on the bathroom floor.

She kisses the photo. The pain is hitting harder, harder in her chest. She tries to open her mouth to call out his name, but it is as if a hand closes over her opening lips. Blackness overwhelms her and a suffocation.

THE MARTYRDOM OF ALYOSHA

The café in St James's Street is not as frequented as some others in the street by hipsters, students or ageing people trying to keep up with the trends. It is a simple café, kept alive by people who do not consider themselves to be in any particularly desirable category. Dmitri sits at a small plain table by the window, waiting, and once or twice he looks at his watch. The man he is waiting for is late and he wonders if he will come at all. He has never met him before, but has a text description of what he looks like: medium height, dark close-cropped hair, dark eyes. The door of the café opens and a camp young man comes in, smudged eyeliner around his eyes and a tired expression that says he has not slept properly for days. He orders a coffee to take away and Dmitri wonders if he has come from the bar further down the street where men in drag hang out, often on the street itself.

"Thanks, love."

The camp young man turns away from the counter and, as he leaves, gives Dmitri a pleasant smile. Dmitri's first thought is that he would not be allowed to behave like that in Russia.

"Hello."

He looks up. The text description is right. This is the man he has been waiting for.

"You must be Dmitri."

The voice is low, as if afraid that people around will hear. It is a tone of voice often heard in Moscow, especially in places where gay men meet. A voice that still sounds afraid, even in Brighton. It is a tone used to the possibility of betrayal and violence.

"And you must be Yuri. Sit down."

They sit side by side at the window and Yuri stares out at

the late spring day, looking in silence for a while at the diversity of people passing by.

"I am sorry I am a little late," he adds after a while. "The bus took for ever. I think there are far too many buses in Brighton. Around London Road it was impossible. This city is not able to cope with all that traffic, is it?"

They are speaking Russian and Dmitri wonders how to begin a real conversation.

"Why did you choose this café," he asks, turning to face Yuri.

"I used to come here often when I first came to Brighton. It is more like the places I used to go to in Moscow. Simple. You know. No pretensions. Ordinary people. This place reminded me of home."

Dmitri smiles at him. He is not sure yet, but he thinks he likes the man. He also finds him attractive, especially his dark skin and hair, but this is not the reason the arrangement was made to meet. He tries to estimate the man's age. Late twenties perhaps, although he looks older. He looks as if he has experienced too much.

"How did you find my number?" he asks.

Yuri stares down at his hands, spread flat on the table. Dmitri notices he has long fingers, and with the usual Russian tendency to romanticise, he thinks they look like the hands of a pianist.

"I was given a book. Alyosha's personal contact book in Moscow. It was after—" Here he stops and his hands clench into fists. He looks up and stares again out of the window.

"Then why didn't you contact me when you first came to Brighton? How long has it been since you arrived?"

"Three months."

"And in all that time you didn't ring or send a message?"

"The pain was too fresh."

The words come out, precise and clear. His voice is louder as he says this. Then he turns and faces Dmitri. His eyes have a feverish look in them and Dmitri sees only too clearly that the pain is still very much there. He reaches out and places one of his hands on Yuri's. The sudden contact brings a smile to Yuri's lips and he says softly, "Let's not order anything. The late afternoon is fine. The pier is a good place to walk, and among all the people, it is possible to be alone. I think I like the pier best of all."

There is just the hint of a child talking when he speaks. A child that has had its emotions broken, but who still needs and wants to play.

"We can have something to drink there. Somewhere in the sun, facing the sea."

"Yes, let's do that."

He is making Dmitri feel young. For a moment, all thoughts of Alyosha are gone. He is a young man with another young man. This could be a date, but it isn't, and it is a nice thing for a moment to pretend that it is. As he gets up, he glances at himself in a mirror on the wall. His blond features are wider, more Slav-looking than Yuri's.

"Let's go," he says.

On the pier, they sit at a silver topped table facing the west. Yuri goes away for a few minutes and returns with two plastic cups of coffee. They sip at the coffee in silence for a while, gazing at the people passing by. Beyond the moving bustle of life, they can just perceive the movement of the waves. The sea is very calm, and the small thin waves are not going directly to shore, but are edging sideways towards the east. Yuri turns to face Dmitri and asks if the sea is afraid of approaching the shore.

"It is one of those phenomena that can happen," Dmitri replies. "Today they have chosen to go towards the east, on some other days it is the west."

"I find it beautiful," Yuri says, "beautiful and strangely reticent. It is peaceful and gives the impression of denying force."

He covers his face for a moment with his hands. Dmitri

looks at him, seeing beyond this image, another image. He sees a pale young man with light brown hair lying foetus shaped on the ground, his slender fingers covering his face with both hands. He is surrounded by feet. Feet in sneakers and boots and soft suede turned hard, poised and ready to kick in. To kick the body; to break open the hunched-in foetus shape. To kick the body until it is forced lengthwise; until it is forced to relax its defending hands. Dmitri shakes off the image from going further and hears his voice saying, "Are you alright?"

Yuri lowers his hands. His eyes look a little red, as if they have fought off tears.

"It is the sun. It suddenly blinded me. Only for a moment."

Dmitri gives Yuri the plastic cup and Yuri, smiling, takes it from him and drinks slowly.

"I saw him for a moment," Dmitri says. "I saw him on the ground, trying to ward off the blows. That terrible photo of him, taken at the demonstration, surrounded by the vigilante group."

"He was once your lover," Yuri replied. "I was once his friend. You were lucky not to have been there. To have been impotent, as I was, and unable to help him because of the brutal crowd."

"I didn't know you were there."

"Yes. Only a few steps away, but I could not get to him in time. His face was bloodied and his clothes filthy with their boots when I at last managed to get through."

Yuri gets up and goes to the railings of the pier. Waiting at the table, Dmitri is undecided whether to go and stand beside him. Yuri seems very distant, caught in a shaft of direct sunlight which seems to form a halo around his body. Then at last Dmitri goes to him, caught too in the strong heat of the sun's blaze.

"Do you mind if we stand here?" Yuri asks. "I don't want to see those people for a while. I just want to look at the quiet water."

"Yes," Dmitri says simply.

"I expect you want me to fill in the gaps you do not know about," Yuri says softly. "If you are not too tired, let's just stand here and I will tell you as much as I know."

"Anything that makes it easier for you," Dmitri replies.

"We both loved him, didn't we? You in your way, me in mine. Alyosha. It is very hard for me to say his name, even now without crying out."

There is a pause. A cheeky seagull decides to perch on the railing near to them and edges sideways along the rail towards them. Yuri turns to look at the bird and remarks on the clean whiteness of its wings, and on the strange beauty of its glinting eyes and curve of beak.

"I love them," he says. "I wish we had bread. I usually carry a little bread for them, but I forgot today."

Dmitri notices the gentle tenor of Yuri's voice, much lighter now after having momentarily moved away from the subject of Alyosha. He wants to reach out with his hands to touch this stranger who is now no longer a stranger. He wants to talk to him of other things: of things that will make him laugh, perhaps make him happy. At least for a while.

"Seagulls always make me happy," Yuri says, as if echoing Dmitri's thoughts.

"Me too," Dmitri replies.

"But they can be vicious too when they see a prey that they want. I have seen them fight among themselves."

"I like to think, Yuri, that they are not like us men. They do not appear to arouse as much terror in each other as we do."

"Yes, I know what you mean." And then Yuri says *yes* again. This last *yes* sounds definitive. Yuri stares out towards the other ruined pier and begins to talk about what happened in Moscow.

"He was taken away by the police," he says. "Alyosha disappeared for quite some time, and when at last, a month later, I caught up with him sitting on a bench in Gorky Park, he looked older, beaten. The bruises had faded from his face, but there was a scar on his right cheek. He made movements with his hands to cover it while we were talking, as if he was ashamed of it. After we left the park and walked along by the river he was silent most of the time. He did not mention what the police had done to him, or how he had suffered at their hands. Only once did he say something direct about his experience and even then it was not directly about the incident at the protest or his arrest. He just looked at me and in a whisper said, 'I will not live much longer. I know what will happen.' I shudder when I think of those words. I wondered how he could have such a presentiment and what made him sound so sure."

Yuri paused. The light was beginning to fade over the sea just slightly. Towards the west, the sun in its rounded shell looked violent in its vivid red.

"He did die then?" Dmitri asked, already knowing. "I wasn't sure. I left Russia almost immediately after my relationship with Alyosha ended. He was more political, and at the time I was afraid. I was afraid that joining him in his political views and activity would destroy me. I suppose I was a coward."

"We are all cowards in our own different ways," Yuri said as if he wanted to defend Dmitri in his perception of himself.

"But you stayed, Yuri. You went with him to protest. You stood up for our right to live our lives in Russia. You did not run away."

"I would have, if I could have afforded it. My English is good and I had links in this country that would have made it possible."

"I am sure it was not only money that stopped you."

Yuri began to shiver. The sun was now sliding down rapidly and a cold breeze was blowing in from the west.

"Let's walk back to my place," Dmitri said.

"Where do you live?"

"In a flat share in Hove. It's at the top of a house. Two bedrooms and a shared living room. I share with a straight guy who knows I'm gay, but he doesn't mind. I rarely see him he works so hard."

"And you?"

"Yes, I work hard. My technology degree helped me get a good job here. Enough to make a life before I decide if I want to return to Russia in the near future, or wait for better times."

"You may have to wait quite a few more years," Yuri says sadly. "The tide there is not about to turn any time soon. Hatred, and complicity in hatred of the other, runs too deep." He paused, then added, "Yes, I would like to come to where you live."

In his apartment in Lansdowne Road, Dmitri makes tea and Yuri leans back on the living room sofa. The place is clearly expensive and has all the polish of an hotel suite passing itself off as a flat.

"When does your flatmate return," he asks.

"I expect he is with his girlfriend. She lives in her parents' house on Dyke Road. He is not very well off and will probably marry her for her money."

"That sounds cynical."

"Yes, I suppose it does, but he told me this himself. Of course he loves her as well."

"Of course."

Yuri takes his tea, this time, served up in bright, expensive cups. Dmitri joins him, but does not sit beside him. He desires Yuri, but in an obscure way it seems a betrayal of Alyosha. He sits in a chair facing him. The tall pointed ceiling of the attic has the feel of a secular cathedral as well as of an hotel.

"Can I be honest?" Yuri asks.

"Yes."

"I do not like this flat."

Dmitri laughs. He senses a simplicity in Yuri that was similar to Alyosha's. He realises suddenly that this was why Alyosha and Yuri had been friends and not lovers, and why as an opposite, he had been a lover suitable for Alyosha. Then he dismisses his thought as being the dismal psychology that in all probability it was.

"Did you love him very much?" Yuri asks abruptly.

"Yes, but I think sometimes not enough."

"What is enough?" Yuri smiles and reaches out to put his cup on a low coffee table.

"Enough to have stayed, like you."

"These seem like the self-flagellating words of the Orthodox church. To always demand too much of oneself, even in love, is a sort of masochism. I am sure Alyosha was satisfied with the gift of time he had with you."

"Did he ever mention me?"

"Yes. Often. You marked his life in a good way. If you hadn't I would not have come to see you. Perhaps I would never have come to Brighton to live."

"I did not ask about where you live. That must seem rude. I'm sorry."

Yuri smiles at him and shakes his head slowly.

"Stop blaming yourself Dmitri. We cannot speak of everything in one rush."

"So where do you live?"

"In a studio, off Lewes Road. I like it in that district."

Dmitri smiles at the familiarity of the word district. It reminds him of the various districts in Moscow. He had once lived off the Arbat, near Smolenskaya. Brighton didn't really have districts in the Russian sense and he tells Yuri that.

"We are Russians to the core," Yuri states.

"So who gave you my number?" Dmitri asks.

For a while Yuri is silent, then leaning back on the sofa with closed eyes, he replies, "Anton. Anton Simonov. I did not know him before, and I certainly did not know what he had done."

"What do you mean?"

Yuri opens his eyes and stares hard at Dmitri.

"You will not like this."

"Don't make a mystery of it. Just tell me."

Again a long pause. Light has faded from the sky. Dmitri gets up and turns on the side lamps.

"He was one of Alyosha's tormentors. He was one of the boys in the group responsible for his death,"

"What?" Dmitri almost screams out the word.

"Sit down. Be calm, for my sake as well as your own. Anton Simonov was a very quiet boy I think, who felt very guilty about being in the vigilante group that followed Alyosha to his apartment building off Pushkinskaya."

"So that is where it happened?"

"Yes."

Dmitri sits down and begins to shiver, not with the cold of the spring evening, but with the coldness that signals the onset of an illness. He knows that what he is about to hear will make him ill.

"Can I sit beside you?" he suddenly asks.

Yuri nods his head and a gentle smile appears on his face. When Dmitri sits next to him he reaches out with his arm and draws Dmitri towards him, hugging him for a moment, not in a sexual way, but with the familiarity of a brother who senses his brother's chill and wants to warm him.

"Alyosha knew he was being followed," he began. "It was a slow—how can I use such a religious word, but it is true—a slow martyrdom. To so many Russians, all gay men are paedophiles, otherwise, why should this group call itself *Occupy Pedofilyaj*? The police I believe were complicit and so was the corrupt grapevine of knowledge about the whereabouts of known gays."

Dmitri moves away from Yuri. He does not need any touch now, any contact. He wants to be alone within himself as he listens.

"The bastards," he says.

"Call them what you like. I simply call them men. They work with the state and the church, but they are men, cursed by hatred. Anton was one of them, but unlike them, I believe he had a conscience. He knew what he had participated in, what he was guilty of. He had watched as they encircled Alyosha outside his door. He had helped as they pushed him inside. He was there when they stubbed cigarettes out on his body. He was there when they at last, mercifully, strangled him and then pissed on his dead body."

"Stop. Please stop."

"Just one more fact. I forgave Anton. Don't ask me why. I cannot explain it. He gave himself up to me. He asked me to kill him for what he had done, but I told him that his death would be living with it."

"I could not have done that."

"I am not you, Dmitri. Perhaps I was a coward to do so. It takes a certain strength to hate that much: to hate so much we cannot forgive. If it is cowardice then I am guilty of letting Anton Simonov go. He also gave me a notebook. It has all of Alyosha's telephone numbers and contacts in it. Plus a photo of him with you."

Dmitri cries as he hears this, crumpling up into a chair.

"Anton took it from Alyosha's body. He was the last to leave the room and the last to leave Alyosha. Like the others he had urinated on him, but unlike the others he stayed behind, and as he put it, in a state of shame."

Dmitri dries his eyes and moves restlessly around the safe living room. No tormentors would break in here; not here in the safe district of Hove, so cut off from the mainland of the world. He feels the full horror of his safety and wraps his arms around his body, uselessly mimicking a holding in love that he feels is gone forever from him. He watches Yuri as he paces, and sees him place the black notebook on the small low table. He cannot face as yet the image of himself with Alyosha. He has no idea how long it will be before he is able to do so. Yuri is talking in the background. All of life is now in the background. The shock attacks him, wave after wave of hot boiling water. It is as if he is drowning in the knowledge of what he has heard. Then very slowly the words Yuri is saying infiltrate into his mind, and in listening to them, the waves recede, and only the slow drip of what Yuri says remains.

"I have been to some of the churches here," Yuri says. "The Catholic ones. It is true they are not as vociferous in their hatred as our Orthodox church, but as long as we homosexuals reject their celibacy they will continue to kill. They kill with the hatred of silence, even though their words are not meant to inspire actual killings. This is the only difference between them and the Orthodox. They say they do not approve of the barbarity in Russia today, but what of what happens here? What of the boys and men and women who commit suicide because of self-hatred? Did you know there is a tree in St Ann's Well Gardens to commemorate them? No one desecrates it, but at one of the entrances to the park, someone has burnt off the words *LGBT memorial tree*. It is a small violence compared to what happened to Alyosha, but it is on the same path. The churches here, like in Russia, hate our physical expression of love."

Dmitri goes towards Yuri and sits beside him. He draws close to him and this time Yuri does take him in his arms.

"There are even some priests who publicly express their personal disgust of anal sex. Disgust is at the core of their man-made theology." He pauses, his voice near to breaking by the emotion he is feeling. "And Alyosha died for his supposed sins. Was murdered for them. He is a crushed face among so many other crushed faces, killed by henchmen tolerated by the church and state. Even the rule of law, when imposed, gives those killers minor sentences if caught. But I tell you, Dmitri, if God exists I wonder if He will have mercy towards his representatives: those representatives of Christ on earth? If God exists, He will love that boy for what he was, and perhaps in the world beyond the grave, for what he still is. But I wonder if God will forgive the church as I forgave Anton?"

As he said these last words, Yuri moved his head closer to Dmitri and their mouths met in a kiss.

MEMORY CITY

He returned to the city, remembering. Fourteen years before, he had made the same journey. Then, he had intended to spend the rest of his life there. Give up all he knew of England and throw in his lot with a country where he understood neither the language nor the customs. He remembered the small amount of luggage he had brought with him. Two suitcases. One with his favourite books and music, the second with his clothes. He had sold up everything else and given the rest to charity shops. It had been a great adventure for him and he had made so many promises to himself that he would make it work. His parents had both died within the space of a year, from cancer, and he had been left a substantial inheritance: enough to start a new life and to give up his job as a manager of a men's clothes shop. At fifty-two he was well beyond the age of caring about men's new fashions, and he had only stayed on with the firm because he had been too lazy to look for something else. His parents' death had been his liberation and he took that freedom almost greedily in both hands. This reclusive middle-aged man who had lived only in books and fantasy could now move on and taste life itself. The flat he rented was easily left behind and so were the very few friends he had made over the years. He had often thought that constitutionally he wasn't made for friendship. He was not a good listener to other people's problems, and he was shy about talking of his own. The day he had left with his two suitcases, no one had really cared.

As he remembered, he saw his former excited self, get off the train at Amsterdam Centraal, feeling forty-two instead of fifty-two and quite ready (or so he thought) for anything that life here would give him. He knew exactly which hotel to stay in as he had stayed there before. It was on Kerkstraat, and faced two beautiful old buildings, twins, dated 1697. He asked for the room he liked and as good luck seemed to be with him, it was free. Standing at the window looking out at the twin houses, he unpacked his things. He tidied his clothes neatly away, then stacked his books by his bed and on a shelf above it. His pile of CDs came next, and he promised himself that the following day he would go out and buy himself a small CD player. He looked forward to the times when he would be alone in the hotel room, playing his music (especially Lutoslawski's Third Symphony which he had just discovered). Then he decided that he was not, absolutely not, going to settle into the same routines that he'd had in England. Amsterdam was his new life, his new city, and didn't he have to find a flat to rent, and courses to join so as to learn the language?

That first evening fourteen years previously, he stayed in and had a meal in the restaurant downstairs. The hotel was Czech run and he enjoyed talking to the waiter who was friendly and helpful. He heard all about Prague and how it was as beautiful as Amsterdam. He made a mental plan that after he had settled he would go there for a few days. Amsterdam would be a stepping stone to other places. In his mind there was no end to the possibilities.

"If you're not too tired, will you take a drink with me after the restaurant is closed?"

The young waiter whose name he could no longer remember (but let's call him Karel) had asked him this as he handed him the bill.

"How nice of you to ask," he had replied with a slightly formal smile, and more than a slight worry that Karel would impose upon him with problems about his family in Prague, or his relationships in Amsterdam. This first night, he didn't want to think about anything else but his own future, his own expectancies. All the same he said his formal, "Yes."

"What time do you finish?" he asked.

"The restaurant closes at ten. Give me half an hour." And then the hesitant request, "Shall I call for you at your room?"

Instead of yes, he said no, and asked if he could wait for Karel in the closed restaurant. Karel looked awkwardly at him, murmuring that he supposed that would be alright with the owners, and asked him to tell anyone who came in that the restaurant was definitely closed.

"Leave a light on and a hungry visitor can be very persistent." He said this with a rather petulant pout, and moved away hurriedly to clean the other tables. Then just as suddenly he turned and asked, "I am stupid. I have forgotten your name."

"Joseph."

Karel muttered that he had a cousin called Joseph, and that it was a nice biblical name, then he resumed his obsessive cleaning of tables that didn't appear to need cleaning at all. When he looked up, Joseph had gone back to his room.

Once inside with the door shut and locked (afraid of some aggressor?) he had sat down on his bed and opened a book to read. It was a book by Charlotte Brontë, *Villette*, and with a sigh close to regret, he put the book aside. It was a complex book and hard to read, yet he enjoyed its complexity, but all the same he had to remind himself he was no longer in his quiet flat in his quiet English town with his quiet books, but in an exciting place with so much potential. Karel, after all, was already potential. He really hadn't needed to be quite so grudging in his acceptance of a drink. This was what he had come to the city for: to meet people and to exchange experiences. Meeting people was exchanging experiences. He had better accept that fact. And so, while he was waiting to go back down to the restaurant he had a long bath and lay in the water until it became tepid, thinking of all the exciting things that would inevitably (if he permitted them) happen to him. He took so much time dreaming about this that it was half past ten when he got out of the bath. Karel would be waiting in the restaurant, and he still wasn't ready. But then again, if he had accepted Karel's request to come to his room, he would have been naked on the bathroom mat and that fact would have hurried him into thoughts of actual experience, long before he was ready for them. In his stupidly confused mind, he recalled the words, by Shakespeare, that *the readiness is all*.

"You are here."

Karel looked impatient. It was a quarter to eleven.

"I had a problem with the bath."

"Is it not working?"

"Slowly. The water was slow."

"We must get a plumber."

"Please, it wasn't that slow."

"But others in the hotel might be inconvenienced. The owners would not want complaints."

"Maybe it is only in my room. The other rooms are probably alright."

"Wait here. I will go into number eleven, which is free, and check."

So much for lying. He waited while Karel checked the water in number eleven, and had to listen to the obvious answer that the water was flowing as fast as it should.

"As I said, maybe it is only in my room," he said feebly. Then he tried to smile away the foolish, unnecessary turn of conversation by asking where Karel had in mind.

"It's just across the street. A small bar, but very friendly. I use it a lot."

He wondered if Karel had chosen the bar because it was nearby, near enough to offload him if necessary, or because he really did have a fondness for it.

Once in the bar, sitting beside Karel on a stool he looked around. It was a long corridor of a place, and behind the bar was an impressive display of liqueurs collected from different countries. He wondered if they were for consumption or merely decoration and asked Karel what he wanted to drink.

"Please. I asked you." Then a slight and very polite pause. "What would you like?"

"A beer."

Karel looked at the bartender, whose name was Cees.

"A beer, and my usual white wine."

After a to-ing and fro-ing of 'what kind of beer?' the night settled into itself. He leant back as far as he could on the stool without falling, and looked at Karel. Karel was a handsome man in his late twenties. Out of his waiter's uniform, he could judge him as a person, and not just as the friendly waiter who had been nice to him that evening.

"So Joseph, what do you expect from Amsterdam?"

The bartender who was rather old and fat looked as if he wanted to stay and listen to the answer, but Karel gave him such a sharp look that he quickly moved away.

"I'm not sure. I think I want to live here for a while."

"You must be very free."

He heard this sentence as if it were a sentence of death. The word *free* had never sounded so frightening. In his mind he was suddenly perched on a very precarious crag up a tall mountain and quite suddenly there was no immediate way down.

"Free?" he questioned. "Yes, I suppose I am. It's funny to say this—" he stopped. It was not funny to say this at all. He had wanted freedom from his old life and now, because of a liberal amount of money, he had it. It was no longer an abstract desire in a claustrophobic English town, but a very real thing he had to face. The excitement of it all suddenly faded into fear.

"I feel as if I am up a tall mountain with too much of a view, and no way as yet to get my feet on the ground."

"That is interesting."

"Is it?"

He looked with alarm at the other men in the bar. How many of them were as free as he was? Was Karel free? He wanted to rush back to the safety of his hotel room and force his way back into the comfort of a nineteenth century novel. Then he breathed a sigh of relief as Karel appeared not at all concerned to pursue this line of conversation. Clearly he had not come out to hear about mental mountains, or of men who did not have their feet on the ground. It seems that he had quite simply needed a simple drink and the simple company of a man who was not in need of going too deeply into things.

"You must forgive me, Karel. I'm a little tired after the journey, and maybe a little light-headed. I did drink more than I'm used to at dinner. Mind you, your Czech beer is excellent."

"Yes, we get it twice a month from Prague. My brother brings it over in his car. We are the only people in Amsterdam who have it."

The conversation flowed into safer waters. He was no longer asked what he intended to do with his time, or his life in Amsterdam, and there was no repetition about expectations. Indeed the conversation was so boring that the bartender stayed away from them altogether, and before a second drink was even mentioned, Karel excused himself, said that he had forgotten to do something really urgent and left the bar.

Alone. He was alone. Everyone around him was speaking Dutch, and as he only understood the fewest of words, he didn't feel a part of the crowd. This was freedom indeed, and he ordered vodka this time, to take the edge off this uneasy thought.

"You like vodka?"

He was surprised to hear English. He was astonished that someone was even questioning him. He turned his head towards the sound of the unexpected voice. A very pretty young man was smiling at him. Full set of white teeth, and clothes that screamed of a fashion he certainly had not seen in his English town.

"I am Boris."

His immediate thought was what a dark name for such a pretty person. With the slightest of hesitations he replied that he was Joseph. This was clearly enough of an invitation and soon pretty Boris was occupying the stool beside him. Immediately the bartender was in front of them and, without a word, was pouring a second vodka, this time for Boris.

"Seems he knows your drink."

"I am a cliché Russian. Of course I like vodka. Now, are you ready for another?"

With a light voice that carried itself with the strength of a bell, Boris got the bartender back and asked him to pour out another vodka. The rather subdued crowd of Dutch men around them were now all looking in their direction.

"You are not Dutch. I heard you speaking to that waiter from across the street."

"Karel."

"Is that his name?"

This was said with some contempt. Joseph noticed the difference immediately. He was not sure he liked the new company he was in, but the part of him he should have ignored wanted the young man to stay. Suddenly he was no longer alone, and his frightening freedom was momentarily filled with the prospect of some real, if not totally wanted, excitement.

"I am English."

"Which place in England?"

"Worthing."

Boris said that he didn't know it, which came as no surprise.

"You in business?"

"I was in business."

"What?"

He had the impression that things were being rushed a bit, but all the same replied, "Clothes."

"I like clothes."

"So I see."

Boris flashed his perfect teeth, and then looked down at the leather jacket and the bright shirt he was wearing.

"I bought these in Paris. I have just come back from Paris."

Nothing Boris said seemed to expect much of an answer, so he did not get one. Then came a rather long monologue about a modelling job that had not materialised, and a series of disappointments that had led him to Amsterdam.

"You must be very free."

He was glad to toss that question back at someone. He felt as if a weight had been lifted from him. Maybe freedom was not such a heavy burden after all.

"I could not live if I wasn't free."

"But Russia—"

"—has changed."

The words were immediate, and he was silenced from asking anything about Russia. What Boris then said carried on for a good hour or so. Nothing that was spoken of was troubling, and it came as rather a shock when the bartender said it was closing time. He felt more than slightly drunk. He was in fact very drunk indeed, and the prospect of going out into the cold night (it was the dull month of February that he had chosen to come and stay) was not welcome at all. He had found a new place of safety in the bar and he liked the taste of vodka, which could, he knew, if he allowed it, become an addiction.

"You have an hotel?"

The pretty features of Boris had become somewhat blurred. He looked at him almost shyly and said, "Yes." The spirit of adventure was rising in him. The bar was emptying fast around them, and the bartender was becoming irritable.

"It's time. It's time please for you all to go."

Was the bartender speaking in English, or was Boris translating for him? There was a hurry, and he had to make a decision. Should he let the adventure pass him by for tonight, or should he give in and allow anything that was going to happen, happen? After all, he was far away from England, and Boris could be a baptism of sorts for his arrival in Amsterdam.

"I am in the hotel across the street."

"You like it there?" Boris asked. "You really like it there?"

"What's wrong with it?"

Boris shrugged. He was wrapping a scarf around his neck, and seemed to have no intention of saying any more.

"Do you want to come back there with me? I haven't any drinks in the room. I think I've had enough drinks for tonight, but if you feel you want to continue drinking I can always ask the bartender to sell me a bottle."

Boris shrugged again, tightening his scarf higher around his neck. Joseph turned away from Boris and tried to get the attention of the bartender who was talking to a group of old men at the farther end of the bar. At last he was noticed and he came over.

"Yes?" No smile. While he said the single word, he was looking at Boris.

"I would like to buy a bottle of vodka."

The bartender, still looking at Boris, snapped out the words, "Is it for him?"

He felt like saying that this was none of the man's business, but made a feeble reply that he was still thirsty. The bartender laughed and walked away without another word.

"He is being deliberately rude. Why should he be rude? He doesn't know me."

"I will ask him," Boris said.

Tired, drunk and feeling frustrated that the night was ending on an unfriendly note, he let Boris take control.

"Cees, come on, you have a bottle to sell. He will pay what you want for it."

Bending down behind the counter, Cees brought out a bottle of vodka, and coming back to them, slammed it down on the bar in front of him. The price was high and Boris turned to Joseph questioningly.

"Do you want to pay as much as that?"

Joseph produced the money, not caring, as long as he could get out of the place. In his confused mind the bar was no longer a place of warmth, or of safety, but savage, lonely, and alien. The bartender took the notes without thanks, and coming round to their side, quickly hustled them out of the door and onto the street. The cold wind hit him in the face.

"It's over there."

He pointed to the hotel with the hand that held the bottle. Boris sarcastically said that he had been told that already, and they crossed the road to the entrance. Once inside he caught a glimpse of Karel in the shadows: just the briefest of glimpses. He felt he had been watching and waiting for him. He remembered this very clearly now and wondered why he had not perceived it as an omen, but then, it was fourteen years ago and incredibly, he still had to invent a name for the man who had caused him so much trouble.

Boris had seen him as well and murmured, "He doesn't like me."

There was a story there, but he was feeling too tired to hear it. He wanted to be alone with Boris in his hotel room and to get what comfort he could from the rest of the night. Once inside the room, he felt giddy and sick. Rushing to the adjoining bathroom, in case he was going to vomit, he caught a look at himself in the mirror. The image was blurred and not very pleasant. He was neither sick, nor able to urinate, which he desperately wanted to do. I am not functioning, he thought, and returned to the room to find a naked Boris waiting for him on the bed.

"I don't know why you chose this hotel. If you can afford Cees's vodka, you can afford better than this."

"I have been here before."

"How unfortunate," was the sudden sarcastic reply.

He made no attempt to answer it, and with giddiness returning, he removed his clothes unsteadily, but methodically. The trousers, neatly over a chair, followed by the shirt and the sweater, and then the inevitable underwear. He had only been to bed with about four other people in his entire life, and the worrying thought came to mind that he wasn't going to get much out of this.

The room was overheated, and they stayed for about an hour on top of the duvet, tumbling about like amateur wrestlers, trying to work up some enthusiasm. Who penetrated who? Or had they both penetrated each other? The sport between them was hasty, brutal and hard, and when the exercises were over Boris quickly leapt from the bed and got dressed. He named his price. The transaction was terminated with some sort of clarity, and he was alone once again in the hotel room. Almost at once, he fell into an exhausted sleep.

Two days later, after a long and bitterly cold walk around Amsterdam he returned to the hotel to find there had been a disaster. A disaster concerning him. To be precise, he had been robbed of all the money he had stupidly left in the room, and most of his CDs and clothes were gone. He remembered his first reaction was one of surprise that anyone would want to steal his unfashionable clothes. Then he counted up in his mind the hefty amount of guilders he had lost and nearly cried. This had been his cash deposit to put down on an apartment. He would have to get more money from England.

"The police," he mumbled. "Have the police been told?"

The owner of the hotel said he thought he knew who the culprit was, and had called the police. They would be round soon.

"Who was it?"

Karel's name was given.

"Why?"

The question hung in the void, and the owner looked away and hunted through a pile of letters on his desk. How could such an obvious question be answered? A need for money, and goods to sell. Wasn't it obvious? Or was this stupid foreigner just going out of his way to be even more stupid? He sensed all this as he stared at the owner, and he sensed too the futility of trying to find answers. Intuitively he knew that Karel had targeted him and had got even for some unspoken rejection or jealousy that had occurred two nights before.

"How do you know it was Karel?" he insisted.

"He is gone. His room is empty. The police will no doubt find his fingerprints in your room."

"But he is part of your family, isn't he?"

The owner laughed at him. In the cold light of that terrible day he had laughed in his face.

"Family? That arrogant little queer? He was certainly not part of my family. We only took him on because we needed extra help and generously let him stay. The last homo we employed here was the same. A thief. They're all liars and thieves."

He had walked away from the owner, and sat as far away as he could from him, waiting for the police to come. Of course, when they did, they tried to appear helpful, but thefts of this kind happened all the time, and the implicit inference was that somehow it had all been his fault. Hadn't he admitted to having a late night drink with Karel in that gay bar? The owner gave the questioning officer a wink which was followed by a direct question: whether Karel had ever been welcomed into his room before the theft.

"I didn't know him like that."

"Like what? We didn't ask you how you knew him, but whether he had the excuse to come into your room while you were there."

"No," he said. He had gone out with Karel once, and had met up with him downstairs while waiting to go out with him.

Eventually it was over. He didn't want to stay in the hotel any longer. He wanted to get another hotel. He had always thought of this hotel as being gay-friendly, but then again, distinctions were blurred in Amsterdam, and he was not at all clear what they meant by being gay-friendly. Now he would choose an ordinary hotel that had no liberal pretensions. The owner was not sorry to see him go and wished him luck with a smirking smile. He then moved into an hotel near the station. It was bland, and had no objections to any kind of person. A blousy and very fat prostitute was staying on the same corridor as him. Late at night, he could hear her loud orgasms which kept him awake.

Then one evening, he decided to return to Kerkstraat. The bar had just opened. The bartender was different: young and very chatty. He was one of the first people there. He sat on the same barstool he had sat on before.

"New in Amsterdam?" the young bartender asked. He was wiping glasses, and his eyes had the sort of look that wouldn't refuse a drink.

"Yes. I'm thinking of living here."

"You are English. I can tell. Your accent is perfect. I worked in Bath for six months."

He tried to look interested. He didn't like Bath.

"Then I went to Manchester. More friendly. Less snobbish. Bar work. Same as here. I'm Alex. What's your name?"

He said his name.

"Well, Joseph, I may be able to help you. I know this old guy with a large apartment to rent just a few streets from here. Near the flower market. You know where that is?"

He said that he did.

"It's not cheap, but it faces the canal. A really beautiful view of the Singel. I think it's the most attractive canal of the lot."

Then he looked around and yawned and said the bar wouldn't be busy for at least a couple of hours.

"Would you like me to ask my friend more details about the place?"

He invited the young bartender to have a drink with him, and asked for the same vodka he had drunk before.

"I won't have vodka, but thanks for a beer."

They said cheers to each other in the English way, and laughed, and then the man whose name he had instantly forgotten as being Alex, asked him again about the apartment.

"It may be more than I can afford at present," he replied.

He was still bruised from the effect of the theft, and although it had not made a particularly large dent in his capital, he didn't want to show off any more.

"All good Amsterdam apartments are expensive," came the reply and Joseph noticed his lips curl with just the slightest contempt that this foreigner didn't realise that.

"I've forgotten your name."

"Alex."

Now Alex really did look pissed off with him. The yawns became frequent, and soon he found important work to do at the other end of the bar. Joseph sat in the same place, nursing his vodka, deciding that whatever he did that night, he would not get drunk again. Once or twice, Alex came back to ask if he was ready for another drink, but he replied no, he would wait a while.

"I hope it gets busy soon." If Alex had been a cat, he would have swished his tail.

Soon after midnight it did get busy. He sat there and drank his second and then his third vodka. He felt desperately alone and the drink was only increasing his sense of aloneness. He missed England with an aching pain. His missed the clothes shop and the familiar streets. He had absolutely no desire to see this apartment near the flower market. He sensed with despair that somehow it would be another place made in hell, as all places seemed to be in this city. But the city was beautiful. He could not deny that. Then, quite suddenly, out of the corner of his eye, he saw them both: Boris and the waiter Karel together, right at the far end of the bar. He knew they had not seen him. In fact, they were so engrossed with each other that this did not surprise him at all. They were sharing a bottle of vodka. He went through a range of emotions from jealousy to anger and then back again. The spectrum of feeling overwhelmed him. He wanted to go over and hit both of them, but equally, he felt the futility of any action at all. Alex was nearby and in silent pantomime gesture he signalled him to come over.

"Who are those two at the end of the bar?" he asked.

"You mean the young ones?" Alex sneered.

"Yes."

The word felt stale in his mouth, like an admission of failure. He asked because he wanted something confirmed, but then he had seen with his own eyes, so what was there to be said?

"They hate each other and they love each other. One from Moscow, the other from Prague. Both of them bad news. Don't go anywhere near them."

He slid off the barstool and made his way to the door. Alex noticed him going and smiled, then turned automatically to another customer and smiled at him. Once in the street, he realised with overwhelming certainty that he had had enough of Amsterdam. Nothing of any good would happen to him here. The city's brew of good mixed with evil was too potent for him, and with the resolution of positive failure he decided to return to England. It was a young man's world and he felt, at fifty-two, too old for the challenge of the adventures he had anticipated. He would salvage what he could and return to the town he had come from. That decision taken, he packed his now single suitcase and left.

He returned to the city, remembering. But how it had changed and how he had changed. He had spent the past fourteen years, working in the same clothes shop. It was so good that they had taken him back. He had collected new things, and he had even had a relationship for a few brief months. Then time ran out, and his health ran out. The doctor had told him the cancer tests were positive. It was just at the time of his retirement and he had had six months of treatment already. The chances of success were not good, and something inside of him didn't expect them to be. Just one last look at the city I could have made my home, he thought. And here he was, standing again in front of Amsterdam Centraal looking out at a mess of cranes for the construction of a new metro line. It was hot and it was summer. Between the rubble and the mass of people, he moved forward, blinded slightly by the sun.

THE DIRT

"There is something most satisfying about digging in the dirt."

This line of dialogue disturbed me. For the past couple of years, since the turn of the millennium, I had thought myself content, shutting myself in my flat and watching television most of the day. I did not have to go out and plunge myself into the dirty world outside. I had the only life I wanted in my living room, in soap operas, in films, and in mindless quiz programmes. As a character said in one of my favourite old films: *All that Heaven Allows*, "all of human life is there." It was said while pointing at a television set, and here I was following his advice. I was getting my fix of human existence when I wanted it, when I needed it, between meals and during meals. I only went out twice a week to the shops and to walk around the park near the house where I lived. It was enough, and miserable though I was deep down inside, I believed I was content. There I was, curled up on my battered old sofa, cup of tea and some comforting chocolate biscuits nearby, when quite suddenly a woman from the television screen said the words, "There is something most satisfying about digging in the dirt." She was on her knees in a very large garden of the sort that only the rich in this country can afford, and she was scrubbing away at the earth with her hands. It was a typical television soap opera, and the story was of no interest to me at all. I was watching mechanically to pass the time, and yet the words disturbed me. I felt suddenly too clean on that sofa and the disorder of the room around me also seemed to be too clean. I lifted my hands up and looked at them. They too appeared too clean. After all, when I was not watching television, I spent a lot of the time in the bath, lying there to pass the time. I could not remember when I had last been dirty and really in need of a bath. I got up and turned off the television. I paced the room. Why had the words disturbed me? They had been delivered dully, and were a part of a banal script that was not meant to disturb anybody. And yet, they had disturbed me. I looked around the room as I paced backwards and forwards. Everything was in its disordered place, and yet I was not at home in this room. I was a stranger and suddenly felt like an intruder. Why was I here, when I could be outside and seeing for myself what people were doing? I could look at them instead of this room and the other rooms in the flat. Maybe I could again reach down with my hands and touch the dirt that I had kept away from me for so long: the dirt of life itself that I had shut myself away from since my lover's death from AIDS. I had shut myself away and had deliberately avoided life. His death had been atrocious and messy. It had been tangled sheets and long desperate cries. There had been the stench of uncontrolled excrement and sweat. During those days, weeks and months with him I had not taken my eyes away from the scene. I had taken it all in and buried it, and then I had left the mess and the dirt of dying behind me to seek sanctuary in a house of disordered order. The woman on her knees had quite simply told me that it was satisfying, and not terrifying, to experience digging about in the dirt. She had not said earth, which would have been logical considering this was what she was touching, but dirt. The earth itself was dirt, and this was the word that had made me sit up and listen.

I had to go out. I had to see and feel with my senses what a new and fresh digging could mean. I had to pack a bag and go far away from my Brighton flat. Leave England itself for a while and visit an old friend in Paris. I had cut myself off from the people I knew while I was taking care of my lover. My best friend had been hurt, feeling that I had deserted him. Guillaume was the person I needed to see most.

I rang him. I had not rung him in five years.

"Guillaume?"

He asked in French who was calling. He was totally unprepared for my call and showed it. After a long pause he recognised my voice.

"David? Is it you?"

"Yes. A long time."

I was floundering. There was another long pause. He broke it.

"Five years."

"I am sorry."

"It was your decision to shut yourself away. I cannot criticise you for that."

But he was. I sensed that he was, and that he still felt hurt by my rejection of him and my silence.

"I am coming to Paris."

I said the words quickly and easily. Suddenly it seemed the easiest thing in the world for me to leave this familiar space and travel out into the world I had turned away from.

"When?"

"Tomorrow. I will travel up to London tomorrow, then catch Eurostar."

"Have you got your ticket?"

"No," I replied, "but if I have to get a first class ticket I will. After all, I haven't spent all that much money in five years."

"Are you still sick?" he asked.

He meant was I still living on benefits.

"I hardly ever leave the flat. Panic. You know."

"No, I don't know. I never saw you like that."

Silence. I broke it by asking if we could meet up in Paris in a couple of days' time.

"Ring me once you are here," he said.

"That will be good."

He laughed. I suddenly remembered the old laughter and the days when we had studied together in Paris at the Sorbonne. The endless books on writers that he had read for me and that I had read for him. It had been hardworking fun then, and we had enjoyed it a lot. He'd had his own intimate relationships, and I'd had mine. But for most of the time, we kept them in a separate place from our own.

"Isn't it time you thought of working again?"

The question was simple. I had an image of my hands reaching down into something more complex and dangerous than the easy jobs I gave myself around the flat.

"They are not translating many French books into English at the moment."

I made a joke of it. The truth was that after Howard's death, I had been offered several translation jobs. One had been for a gay novel that I had admired in French. The author had wanted me to be first translator of choice.

"We will talk when we meet."

His voice was crisp and almost cold. All the same, I liked to think there was an edge of excitement in it.

"Yes. I hate phones."

"Have you used one in the last five years?"

The question was sarcastic. He suddenly made me afraid. There was absolutely no friendliness in the tone.

"Guillaume, it has been difficult."

"You need not explain."

"But won't I have to in Paris?"

He paused, then I heard him laugh again.

"We will see, in a couple of days' time."

Once the receiver was put down on both sides, I felt cold and scared. I had rung him at his home. Neither of us liked mobile phones. I wasn't even sure he had one. I looked around the room again, desperately needing it to give me some comfort. My hands were wet with panic, but when I looked down at them, I only saw a clean film of sweat. Couldn't even this fear of meeting up with someone again make me the slightest bit dirty? Panic and laziness and the uneasy comfort of my home had given me an invisible armour against dirt.

The following day it didn't take long to see the dirt outside around me. At Brighton station, a black girl was being questioned by four policemen. At first I saw this through a crowd of people, but as I got closer I saw that she was being restrained by them. One was in the process of putting handcuffs on her wrists. She was shouting at them in her own language, and some of them in turn were shouting back at her in English. The scene was violent and then became unbearable as I heard her begin to scream. It was a long and terrible scream. Not like the screams I had heard from Howard, yet they had one thing in common and that was a need for freedom from chains, and for life. A group of people got in the way of my seeing her, and when I had pushed my way through them I saw that she had disappeared. I still heard the screaming, but could not locate where it was coming from. She and the policemen had disappeared. I rushed up to another policeman who was standing impassively nearby. I must have looked threatening, for his immediate reaction was to draw back.

"What has happened to that girl?" I asked.

"Who?"

"Can't you hear her? The girl who is screaming."

"I can't hear it."

"You must be able to hear it. She was having handcuffs put on her. She couldn't speak English, and then she started screaming. She still is. Just listen!"

I said these last two words aggressively. He looked around him, then looked at me and said with equal aggression, "I didn't see anything. I didn't hear anything."

"The arrest," I insisted.

"I don't know what you are talking about. I've told you I didn't see anything. I didn't hear anything."

He repeated those eternal words: those words that have been used by every coward in history who has turned away from a cruel act. Despite his denial I would not let go.

"She has been arrested for something, justified or not.

There were four policemen. She was afraid."

I paused as I was suddenly out of breath. The air was stifling. The summer heat beat down.

"Do they really need four people to handle someone like that?" My voice panted out the words. He looked at me as if I was mad.

"Ask them," he said.

"They have gone."

"Then make a complaint. It's not my business."

He walked away from me, and I felt both frightened for the woman and for myself. Maybe I would have to go back home and give up on the journey. I imagined the police beating her up, or worse, and then I had to sit down and tell myself that I was in England. That the English could not be—and then my mind went blank. Like what? Like human beings? Like people who felt that whatever crime she had supposedly committed she deserved respect? I shuddered. Men in power were men in power. In the hospitals I had seen men hold other men down by force. It was the dirt of the earth in the soul itself, and this is what I had left the so-called safety of my home to experience again.

I got on the train for London. On arrival there, I found a small hotel in Victoria. I could have caught a Eurostar, but out of tiredness, I deferred it to the next day. The room was shabby, and although I felt my habitual need for a bath, I went to bed without one. It was still daylight, but I lay there awake, immobile, staring up at the dirty white ceiling. About midnight, I fell asleep.

My dreams that night made me wake up more than once. There was one especially that recurred. I was in a room, a bedroom that resembled my own in Brighton, and yet it was like no other bedroom I had been in before. Above the bed was a tall grubby window, and the glass in the window was broken at the top. In the dream, I was lying on the bedspread and not between the sheets. I was fully dressed as I was too afraid to get into the bed. I was awake in this nightmare and staring at the broken glass, through which I could see darting creatures, searching for a space through which to enter the room. They droned like bees, and yet I knew that they were something else. Something more deadly, and capable of killing me. Then finally, two of these creatures found their way in and were circling the bed. As they revolved around me, descending slowly, I woke up with a muffled scream. By dawn I was exhausted and got up and sat by the bed. Then I washed my face at the sink, but could not endure getting into the bath. It appeared dark with grime in the light of dawn. I also felt I needed a fresh change of clothes, but feeling too lethargic even to change my underclothes, I picked up my small suitcase and made my way to Waterloo Station. The rush of traffic and the tired faces of morning Londoners disturbed me. I had not been in a crowd so large for so long, and everybody around me appeared run-down. Near to Waterloo, I went into a black and chrome coffee shop and ordered what was for me a very expensive cup of coffee. The people around me there seemed to be no different from the others I had passed in the street. A woman stared at me from a table across from mine. She was thin and shabbily dressed, and although still young, looked old. I felt she wanted to talk, to reach out to someone; to anyone. Moved by her need, I smiled at her, but when I did she turned away her head as if ashamed. A few minutes later she got up and left. I stared at the absent place she had left behind, at the half-drunk cup of coffee and at a crumpled tissue she had left on the table. The buzz of voices around me reminded me of the creatures in my dream and unsteadily I got to my feet and made my way to Eurostar.

The train was packed. I had an aisle seat, which was fortunate as I needed to use the toilet several times. My stomach was churning and I had diarrhoea and a slight but very real incontinence. The smell of my own waste reminded me of Howard and the last time I had been with him while he lay dying. I suddenly desperately wanted a bath and in a panic of frustrated need I tried to clean myself as best as I could standing up at the sink. My underwear felt wet when I sat down, and the disgust at my own soiled self appalled me. The man sitting next to me edged away, and I wondered if I smelt. When we entered the channel tunnel I hurried to the buffet car and had a sandwich. It was the first thing I had eaten in over twenty-four hours. I drank more coffee, then feeling light-headed I made my way back to my seat. I think I slept, for the next thing I knew, I was at the Gare du Nord. I was jostled by the hurrying crowd leaving the platform and someone said something to me in French that I didn't understand because I wasn't listening. The inflection of the voice was urgent though and sounded angry. No doubt I was taking too long to move down the platform.

Once outside on the street I stood still. I was suddenly glad to be back in Paris and took in long, deep breaths. Then I had to make my choice of an hotel and made the easiest one by going into the first that I saw. The people who ran it were friendly and quite soon I was in my hotel room, except this one in contrast to London looked welcoming. After taking a quick shower and changing my clothes I lay down on the bed and fell into a dreamless sleep, overwhelmed again by this endless tiredness. It must have been around six in the evening when I woke up. My first instinct was to ring Guillaume. I used the hotel phone and listened to the ringing of his phone. I waited a long time for a reply, but there was none. Maybe he was in the bathroom. Perhaps he had forgotten that I was coming, but then again, that was ridiculous. Of course he would have remembered that I was coming. I sat in the hotel room for about an hour and tried again several times, but his phone still did not answer.

I spent the evening walking up the Champs-Élysées. When I had lived in Paris I had hated the place, but now I welcomed the gaudy lights of the shops and the pungent smell of perfume coming from *Guerlain*. The atmosphere was totally different from London. The people looked as if they were enjoying themselves, and despite the beggars I felt that the place was not as brutal, not as competitively harsh. Sitting upstairs in a far too expensive café I had something to eat, and it was there that I rang Guillaume again, from the café phone next to an overflowing, stinking toilet. He picked up the phone almost at once.

"David?"

I laughed and said, "Of course."

A long pause.

"David, I don't think I can see you."

Once more my stomach began to churn. Dry-mouthed I asked him why.

"My nephew, Marc, has had a sudden tragedy. I have to be with him. The whole family has to be with him. You may remember me speaking of him. He is my brother's son."

I had never met any of Guillaume's relatives, so of course I did not remember him and neither did I remember Guillaume ever mentioning his nephew: this Marc who was going to prevent me from seeing my friend.

"How long have you known about this?"

I was beginning an interrogation.

"Are you suggesting I am using this as an excuse not to see you, David?" he asked defensively.

"Not at all. I'm surprised you didn't know about the urgency of this when I last called."

He sort of snorted at me down the phone, and the sound was not at all friendly.

"My dear David, you have not changed. Still the same suspicions. When you lived among people and had not separated yourself off from them, you were constantly jealous or suspicious that they were not putting you first."

I looked down at the shabby space I was calling from, so different from the rest of the café. I had been content only a short while ago, up here, drinking, glad to be so close to seeing Guillaume. Now I felt a darkness in the brain, closing off all thought, all action. I could not reply to his words.

"David?"

"Yes."

"I'm sorry. I'm stressed out. I'm worried about Marc."

Mechanically I asked what the tragedy was.

"His wife Sabine has left him. Quite suddenly. My family never approved of her marrying Marc. And now there is another man. She left for America, leaving the children traumatised in Marc's care."

I said it must have been a shock. Then I asked if Guillaume could spare any time at all for me.

"Marc cares for me so much, and the family must come first. It is only normal that it should. Unlike most gays, I believe in the family."

This sounded like a verbal knife that Guillaume had been waiting for the right time to use. I realised how Guillaume had always been ashamed of his homosexuality. He had always revered the so-called 'normal' which he coveted more than anything else. When I lost Howard I had not turned to him. I felt it wouldn't have been a priority for him, and yet, using double standards, he resented that I had closed off and not contacted him. Now I had decided to re-enter the world, it seemed timely for this tragedy. I was ashamed that I did not totally believe in it.

"Are you sure there isn't an hour you could spare me?"

I was begging, and it sounded like it.

"Maybe tomorrow. But if I can, it can only be for a very short time. He is naturally in a state of collapse."

"I know what that feels like," I said.

"What, David?"

"About collapse. I have been there."

"Ah yes, but you chose to go through it alone. Marc rightly feels otherwise."

"In what way, Guillaume?"

"Can you really ask that? When you were social and out there in life, you found people necessary—too much at times, as I said to you when you were here. Also in Paris, you always wanted to turn to me first when things went wrong."

"Howard's death—"

I stopped. I could not go there. I could not talk about it to him.

"Yes? I am listening."

"It changed me, Guillaume. He was so—so great in my life. No help was any use to me after he died."

"Not even from your best friend?"

His voice bit into me. It was meant to bite into me.

"Guillaume, rightly or wrongly I shut myself away, but just before I rang you in England I realised I had to go out again. Out into the world. My first thought then was to you."

"David, there is no time to talk of this. Not on the phone."

"Then where else?"

"I told you, maybe tomorrow."

"Yes, but as you said, the tomorrow is a maybe. I have to let you know why I wanted to return to people. Why I wished to turn to you."

"When did you actually decide on this return?"

"Now. I mean a few days ago."

I felt feverish. My mouth was so dry. The words were like lumps in my mouth.

"Five years is a long time to not make that decision."

"I can't count the years in that way, Guillaume. I can't even fully realise why it's now that I want to get my hands dirty again."

"David, I can hear Marc in the next room. He is on medication. The rest of the family is waiting. I can't stay on the phone any longer."

"Just a few minutes more, please. I rang you because you always understood me before in Paris. I am ready to return to life, and I need your help. I will stay in Paris until you are free to see me. Isn't that making it clear how much I need to see you? I have never stopped loving you as a friend, not even for a moment. I know how you think I rejected your help after Howard's death."

His reply was quiet and cold.

"Have you finished, David?"

"Yes. I am tired."

"So am I. My nephew needs me. He will need me for a long while. You see he must come first. His children too will need extra care. A heterosexual loss has extra terrible consequences that cannot be underestimated."

"I understand," I said.

"I hope so. It was so sudden, so brutal. It is all so cruel."

"Yes. It is."

"Marc was not prepared for it. One day she was there, and then gone, with just a note, justifying it."

"I know about loss."

"Yes but you were prepared for it. You at least had a long preparation before you were separated from Howard. And then, gay relationships don't have quite the same weight of tragedy, do they?"

"But Howard *died*, Guillaume. He *died*."

I was crying by now. Very slowly I shut out the sound of Guillaume's voice. I really did not want to hear him anymore. My hands were wet with tears as I put down the receiver. The summer evening was closing in when I re-entered the café and looked out of the window. All along the Champs-Élysées the lights were very bright and shone clear upon the bright green of the trees. In a short while it would be totally dark. I paid my bill and went out into the street. A distant and very dirty memory had surfaced in my mind while he had said those last words about me being prepared. It was the memory of a night years before when Howard was alive and well. Guillaume had come to stay with us in our flat in Brighton. He had looked around him, and had gone over to the bookshelves and touched the books.

"Do you like books?" he had asked, turning to look at Howard.

Howard had looked young and very awkward. He had admitted when we first met that he was afraid of my French intellectual friends.

"I don't read a lot," he had replied.

"What do you do?" Guillaume asked.

"I play in a band."

Howard had laughed his nervous, boyish laugh.

"And are you successful in your band?"

"We got into the top twenty. For a full three weeks."

"I am impressed," Guillaume had replied sarcastically, then took out a volume of gay short stories. He pretended to be interested in it, although I knew that they were not at all his kind of thing. After replacing the book he had turned to me.

"Well, David, I never thought of you as someone who appreciated popular music. You have changed."

Howard had slipped out of the room.

"You don't like him, do you?" I asked.

"It's not that. I just think you could have done better."

Guillaume was my best friend, and I took the blow he had just given me without flinching.

"He is good for me. In fact he is a good person full stop. It's just you know nothing about him."

I remembered there on the Champs-Élysées that Guillaume had been insistent. He had wanted to be unkind.

"Yes, that's true. But would I respond to what I would have to get to know?" He shook his head slowly. "I don't think so David. When minds are not compatible, I think it makes everything impossible."

He had given me a sharp look, then stared in a mirror and patted at his short black hair. In the mirror I saw that he was looking at me.

"And are our minds compatible?" I had asked.

"They were."

He turned to me as he said this, and then added, "But I am wondering if they still are. A moment ago when I was looking at your bookshelf, I was looking at the Camus I once studied with you. I wanted to bring it off the shelf and show it to you again. Not that silly book of gay short stories which I am sure are inferior to more serious writing. I wanted to ask you if you remembered the essay on *The Fall* that I helped you write. But I stopped myself because Howard was in the room, and I didn't want to embarrass him in case he had never heard of Camus."

I remained silent, and he continued.

"We have to choose rightly, David. Otherwise it ends in disaster."

"And you believe I have not chosen rightly?"

"I don't think that you have. For a week's flirtation perhaps, or maybe a month. But to buy a flat together? To make it a sort of marriage? For that I do not think it was the right choice."

"I am in love," I had said. "It is clean, and it is fresh and it is new. I am in love for perhaps the first time."

"That is simply bad fiction," Guillaume had replied and at that moment Howard had re-entered the room, and the unpleasant, grubby conversation came to an end. Guillaume spent the rest of his stay being coldly polite to Howard, and as he left at the end of his stay I watched as he gave Howard a kiss on both cheeks.

I remembered those days, years before, as if they had been yesterday. I still cried as I walked down the Champs-Élysées to Concorde and then along the Rue de Rivoli until at last I came to Saint Paul. I turned off into the Marais and briefly went into a gay bar. Everyone appeared very young and I felt a stranger among them. One young man tried to pick me up, asking me almost immediately how old I was.

"I'm older than you," I said jokingly.

He turned away, smiling.

I left the bar and made my way back through the painfully familiar streets of Paris until I reached my hotel. Once there I got into bed and to my surprise, slept well. The following morning I caught the first Eurostar back to England, and to whatever else life had in store for me. Two things I was sure of. That I would not return to Paris again, and that I would no longer shut myself away. My stomach was calm the whole of the journey.

PLACE OF DREAMS

He was kicking a ball in St Ann's Well Gardens. Nick watched him, sitting on a seat with his back to the pond. The boy had noticed him and between kicks would look over; it was a smiling, cheeky look that seemed to ask for attention. Nick saw how strong his legs were, and the shorts he was wearing were dirty with mud. The ground was wet with a downpour from the night before and the late autumn grass looked thin and worn after too much use and abuse. The gardens had been crowded all through the summer months, and well into October there had been picnics.

"Do you want to come and join me?"

The cry was cheerful and Nick, feeling self-conscious in his coat and long trousers, shook his head in silence. But he smiled at the boy and raised his hand in a half wave, half gesture of recognition.

"Scared of getting your clothes dirty?"

The boy kicked the ball in Nick's direction and it landed under the long seat he was on. He realised, looking down, that his legs had been wide open, like a goal post. In the next moment, the boy was on his knees in front of him, and without looking up at Nick, retrieved the ball.

"Sorry," he said, looking up. His face was smeared with dirt, but he had bright blue eyes and Nick found them very attractive.

"What's your name?" the boy asked.

"Nick."

"I'm Gregg."

Nick said hello and Gregg sat down next to him.

"I hope it doesn't fucking rain," he said, looking up at the sky. "Always happens at the weekend, doesn't it?"

"I don't come here often at the weekends. I thought there would be more people."

"What do you expect in November?"

"It's warm. The sun's out."

"Not for long. Look at the clouds coming in from Worthing."

Nick laughed. Gregg's voice was much deeper than his, and he was impressed by the forbidden swearword he had used. He wondered if Gregg's parents knew he used words like that. The last time he had used the word 'bloody' he had been hit by his mother.

"Do you swear much?" he asked, turning to stare at Gregg.

"Course I do. Shit, fuck, cunt. Didn't anyone talk like that to you before? Must be a fucking polite school you go to."

"No, they use words like bloody and even shit sometimes."

"Should hope so. Everyone shits. It's the most natural word in the English language. As for bloody, even my seven year old sister says that. It's nothing."

Nick remained silent. He turned away from Gregg and looked at the trees beyond the open space of grass. The trees still had a lot of leaves, but they were turning browner than the earth beneath them. Then quite suddenly he felt a sharp nudge in his side.

"Dressed up like that and sitting like that you look like an old man. I bet you are younger than me, but you look years older."

"I was fourteen a few weeks ago."

"Stand up."

"Why?"

"I want to see how tall you are. Your legs seems quite long, but the rest of you looks shorter."

Feeling embarrassed, but obeying Gregg, Nick stood up.

"Thought so."

"What?"

"You are shorter than me."

Gregg stood and faced Nick. He was about a head taller.

"Does it matter?" Nick asked.

Gregg shrugged, then ran out onto the grass and began kicking the ball again. It was around three in the afternoon and a few people began to appear, most of them walking their dogs. One Alsatian was especially interested in the ball and ran after it when Gregg gave it a second kick. Gregg looked back at Nick who was still standing on the gravel by the seat and called out, "Look, even he is more eager than you are."

"He's a dog," Nick shouted back, stating the obvious. "I'm not as stupid as a dog."

"And he hasn't got a posh voice like you've got. Thank God all fucking dogs bark more or less the same."

The Alsatian, shocked by their shouting voices, bounded away, and running to the ball, Gregg picked it up and returned to Nick.

"Don't you like sport?" he asked.

"It's alright. I don't do much of it."

"What school d'you go to?"

"A small one. You wouldn't know it. Clifton College"

"Posh is it?" He shrugged again. "Oh, fuck it, it doesn't matter. I don't care what sort of school you go to. I never passed my Eleven Plus. I live in Portslade, so I go to the Knoll."

Nick had no idea where the Knoll school was, and as he rarely went to Portslade he had no idea what kind of school it was. Clearly it must be a place that largely ignored swear words, with a big playground, so that in all the noise, the words could not be identified. At his private school they had a small playing area and it was supervised. He looked down at the ground and mumbled that he had better start out for home.

"Where's that?" Gregg asked.

"Montpelier Road. I live in the big red house, next to the tennis court."

"A flat is it?"

"Yes."

"I live in a house. Dad will own it soon. He makes good

money at his electrical shop."

His voice sounded defiant and boasting. There was also an edge of anger in it as if he had to assert something over Nick.

"Why don't we do something?" he said.

"Do you really want to?"

"Don't sound like a sodding wimp. Would I ask if I didn't want to? I know a boy called Charlie. He lives around here. We could go and see if he is in. He's got a TV set. We could see what's on."

Nick, who lived alone with his mother, did not have a TV. She liked the wireless and often in the evenings he would listen to concerts and plays with her. She was separated from his father and lived a solitary life, except for Nick who kept her company most of the time. He certainly couldn't offer to take Gregg back to the flat. None of the kids he knew at school had ever gone back to his place, and as his mother was in ill health, they would not have been welcome.

"I thought television didn't start until the evening," he said.

"Haven't you got a set?"

"We're thinking about it."

"Your mum and your dad?"

"My mother. My father is dead," he lied.

"What did he die of?"

Nick paused. He went through a mental list of illnesses that could possibly lead to death. He knew about pneumonia and cancer and tuberculosis, then he thought of the obvious, the one he wouldn't have to describe any symptoms of.

"Heart attack," he said.

"Was it quiet? I had an uncle who had a heart attack. Bloody cried out as he went, or that's what my dad said. It's supposed to be fucking awful painful."

"I don't know. He died in the street."

The lie was becoming more and more elaborate, but he was ashamed of admitting there had been a separation between his parents. It was almost as shameful as admitting you were illegitimate or that you had been adopted because no one else wanted you.

"Couldn't the ambulance men have saved him if they had come in time?"

"Yes, I suppose so," Nick replied, running out of more ideas for this lie. He had been brought up as a Catholic and had been to a Catholic primary school. Lying was a venial sin, not a mortal one, but all the same, he didn't like to tell them. He might go to Purgatory for that if he told too many and didn't go to confession. Then he suddenly reminded himself, that deep down he didn't really believe God existed. He had realised that in St Mary Magdalen's church one day as he had been gazing around at all the gaudy statues. It all seemed so improbable suddenly, a God up there, way beyond the clouds, paying any attention to him. He had been about eight or nine at the time, and he was so thin and small he thought it would be impossible for a God to notice him, even if He did exist. Then he felt guilty and crossed himself just the same. He was almost tempted to say a few Hail Mary's, but then gave up the thought and looked vacantly at the altar. The priest was raising the monstrance, which was an inappropriate time to look up, and he lowered his eyes quickly. He knew the word 'atheist' as he had been told by a particularly nasty master at school, that atheists were doomed to damnation. He decided there must be a Hell and a Purgatory, and that place Limbo for dead unbaptised babies and for people who had been dead before Christ, and that not believing in God would take him to one of them. He sighed at the comforting thought that he had at least escaped from the possibility of Limbo as he had been baptised. He thought of Heaven without God, then gave up.

"What you so quiet about?"

Gregg's deep voice roused him out of his thoughts. He looked at the boy, then stared down at his sturdy legs. He saw hair growing on them and he felt an impulse to reach out and touch them. He liked hair on men's legs. It was then he realised that he hadn't asked Gregg how old he was. He looked old enough to be as much as sixteen.

218

"Can you get into X films?" he asked suddenly.

Gregg laughed.

"What you asking that for?"

"Don't know. Just wondered."

"I saw my first X film months ago. They let me in. Suppose I look old enough."

"How old are you?"

"Year older than you. Born in December. I'll be fifteen next month."

"So you're fourteen like me."

"I'm not like you at all. Have you got pubic hair yet?"

Nick had pubic hair, but he blushed at the nakedness of the word. It sounded exciting coming out of Gregg's mouth and he felt his penis grow hard. Frightened that it showed, he put his hand down in front of him. Then he remembered he was wearing a coat and it couldn't show through trousers and a coat. He began walking and Gregg moved quickly after him.

"I was just asking," he said. "I know a boy who began growing hair there at ten."

Nick laughed, not believing.

"How do you know?" he asked. He knew this was a daring question to ask, but he had to. His mind was full of images of hair around Gregg's penis, and by asking, he was prolonging what was a forbidden conversation. He also imagined himself being caned for this at school.

"I know 'cos he dropped his trousers and showed me. His cock was bigger than I thought it would be as well. Bloody abnormal, I told him."

They had reached the park entrance on Furze Hill, and it was there that Gregg steered the talk into another area.

"Do you like science fiction comics?" he asked.

Nick liked them very much and told him so.

"I know this shop near the Theatre Royal. In Gardner Street. Want to come with me and look at some?"

"What time does it close?"

"Half-five. We've still got time if we hurry. We won't see

any horror comics like my elder brother has. Fuck knows where he got them from. I saw one once and it had a woman's head being cut off by this monster. It was in colour and there was blood everywhere."

Nick didn't like the thought of this much, but he looked up at Gregg's eager face and noticed again the sparkling, blue eyes. He wouldn't like it at all if there were real monsters and he saw this sudden (and possibly new friend?) having his head cut off.

"Let's run," he said, all too ready to show he was fast at running. He had to begin to impress Gregg.

Brighton and Hove was their playground, from St Ann's Well Gardens to Black Rock. They ran a lot, laughed a lot, and Nick, while he was with Gregg, began to swear as much as he did. Only he wouldn't use the word 'cunt' which he didn't like. A deep reservation made him refuse to use this most forbidden of words. He had heard a drunk in the street say it when he was with his mother, and she had turned on the drunk, a living burning flame of reproval in her red dress, and had said to him, loudly and clearly, "You disgusting man. Aren't you ashamed of yourself?" The drunk had looked at her and laughed through his broken teeth. "What, haven't you got one?" he replied. His mother had drawn Nick quickly away, and they went onto the West Pier where, as she said, "the wind will blow the nastiness and the cobwebs away." Even now, when Gregg used that word, which was less frequent than the others, he looked disapprovingly at him.

"Don't be such a kid," Gregg would say, then pinch him on the arm cheekily and run on ahead.

Every now and then, they would steal comics from the shops in the warren of squalid houses that led down from the station. It was easy to do, especially in the one on Trafalgar Street, where the man who ran it was too blind to see anyway. Gregg would always signal towards the more lurid ones, the ones that resembled the films Nick was too young to see.

One day they sneaked into the back of the shop and the nearly blind man didn't see them. In the back room, they discovered a pile of older comics that were hard-core horror. Some had scantily dressed women being carried by a monster, or a creature, or a thing. He got very confused about why these objects of terror had such different names.

"Why is he called an 'it'?" he whispered as Gregg singled out a comic called *It Came from the Gruesome Lands*.

"It's just to make it more exciting."

"So what is the difference between a creature and a monster?"

Gregg paused and looked reflective, his hand poised to steal.

"Monsters do more," he at last said simply.

Nick felt slightly ashamed at asking such a childish question, then nodded his head in agreement. Since he had met Gregg, he had quickly read both Mary Shelley's *Frankenstein*, which he found very heavily written, followed by Bram Stoker's *Dracula* which was much more to his taste. He pondered a while on this. Frankenstein's creature was called a monster, so it was perfectly clear that you could be both at the same time.

"Can we go and see one of those films?" he asked. "If we're together, I'm sure I can get in with you. You're taller and bigger than me, but you've often said my face looks older."

"After Christmas and my birthday," Gregg replied, then neatly slipped a few of the comics inside his jacket.

"Now let's make a fucking run for it," he said.

The man did not see them as they left the shop, Gregg carrying his forbidden cargo.

Often they would go to see Charlie. He lived in St Michael's Place, which was considered a rough street to live on, with police cars going up and down it. Nick's mother had told him, with inevitable severity, that only drug addicts and prostitutes lived there. She called it low-life and told him he must never loiter near or go along that street. Only bad things happened there.

Gregg laughed when he told him that.

"I bet she got that out of the local paper," he replied.

"She doesn't read the local papers."

"Then she doesn't know nothing," he added, with a full accent on the bad grammar he had learned from detective films on TV.

"She's not stupid."

"Well, don't tell Charlie it's a bad street. His parents had a lot of trouble getting their flat. At first the landlord said he wouldn't take in teenagers. Too much noise for the house, he said, which just shows how quiet the place is supposed to be."

Charlie lived on the top floor of one of the tall houses on the west side of St Michael's Place, almost next to the road which separated it from the more expensive Montpelier Villas. Gregg said there were famous people living there, even someone on television, but he wasn't sure of the man's name.

"Gilbert something," he said. "It's a quiz thing. We don't watch it in our house. It clashes with a programme Dad likes on the other side."

"I don't watch it either," Charlie added, proud of the television set his parents were renting. Charlie was a fat boy who loved sweets which he ate copiously while his parents were out at work. He would often skip school to watch TV, and it was on these days that Gregg took Nick round. He also had a magazine in the bottom drawer of his bedroom which had photographs of nearly naked women in it. He said he'd stolen it from a special shop, but would not say where the shop was.

One day Gregg was bold enough to ask if he and Nick could look at it while Charlie was watching TV in the living room. He had winked at Charlie and given him a big smile. Charlie replied it was okay as long as they were ready for an emergency if his parents suddenly returned.

"What did he mean by that?" Nick had asked, as Charlie

closed the bedroom door behind them.

Gregg said nothing in reply and began to turn the pages of the magazine. He opened it wide to a full double spread of a woman lying on a bed, her hand poised above her groin. She was dressed in a semi-transparent nightdress, which revealed nothing clearly.

"I like this one," Gregg said. He then lay down on Charlie's over-large bed and beckoned to Nick to join him. Nick sat on the edge of the bed and looked carefully at the picture. The woman did not appeal to him at all, but he was aroused by a tension in the air which he knew was sexual.

"What is she about to do?" he asked, his voice a little hoarse with suppressed excitement at what Gregg might say.

"She's about to have a wank," Gregg said quickly. He then looked up at Nick from his own prone position and asked Nick to lie down next to him.

"I don't know how women do it," Nick replied, complying with Gregg's request to lie next to him.

"They finger their cunts," Gregg added crudely. "They put their fingers inside themselves."

As he said this, he began rubbing at his own groin. Nick at first turned away, then getting an erection himself, began to look down at what Gregg was doing.

"I wonder who's got the biggest," Gregg whispered, as if the words were explosive enough to be heard by Charlie in the living room. "Shall I push my trousers down? This picture's got me turned on. Are you turned on?"

"Yes," Nick said, but he was only really turned on at the prospect of seeing Gregg's penis.

"Then let's do it, shall we?"

"Okay."

Nick could hardly breathe he was so tense.

"Take yours out first and show me," Gregg said and turned to look at Nick's face.

"Why me?"

"I want to see if you are bigger than me."

Nick unzipped his trousers, then fumbled with unsteady hands to get his trousers down to his knees. He still had his underwear on, but his erection clearly showed.

"Yeah, I can see you're big. About as big as me," Gregg whispered. He then quickly pushed his own trousers down to his ankles, edged himself up and pushed his underwear down too. His penis was thick and red with blood and he had a thick bush of hair around it. It was the same colour as the hair on his head. Dark brown, almost black.

"I haven't got as much hair as you," Nick said.

"Go on. Show me. Push your fucking underwear down."

Nick did. His penis wasn't as big as Gregg's, nor was it anywhere near as hairy. Gregg looked at it closely.

"Now let's wank and imagine we are both fucking her."

"But you've got the magazine on your side of the bed," Nick said, trying to convince Gregg that this was his real object of desire.

"You've seen her. You can imagine her. Come on, let's do it and no noise, remember? We don't want Charlie hearing us and coming in."

"Have you ever wanked with Charlie?" Nick asked.

"Don't be stupid. I'm not even sure how he finds it in that roll of fat. I don't wank with just anyone."

They both came, almost simultaneously. Gregg looked at the picture most of the time, but sometimes turned to look to see how Nick was progressing. Nick could only concentrate on what Gregg was doing with his hand. Gregg came a few moments before Nick and couldn't suppress a cry as he did. Nick was too far gone to take notice of the cry and was quiet as he climaxed.

"Shit, I hope we didn't get any of it on the bedspread," Gregg said casually, wiping himself down with a dirty handkerchief. "You got one?" he asked, and although Nick did have one, he wanted to touch the wet handkerchief.

"No," he lied.

Nick took it and felt Gregg's wet sperm touch his own

penis. This was the most exciting moment of the afternoon for him, but of course he could not say so.

"You okay?" Gregg asked, pulling up his trousers.

"Yes," Nick said, and clenched the handkerchief tightly in his hand.

Christmas came and went. Nick spent it with his mother and an aunt called Agnes, who was his mother's younger sister. She lived in a remote town in northern England and rarely came down to Brighton. The holiday days passed slowly and he wasn't even much interested in his presents. He was given a watch by his mother and a book by his aunt: a *Rupert* annual which he was far too old for. He kissed her over-powdered face.

"I never can remember how old you are," Agnes said, no doubt suspecting that she should have chosen something a bit older for a boy who had reached puberty. She had considered an unabridged edition of *The Three Musketeers*, but thought the prose looked a bit dense and that the book was, in her terms, far too long.

"He'll soon be a man," his mother had said in one of those rare moments of pride. Nick knew she was secretly longing for him to grow up so there would be a man and not a child to go out with.

After Christmas he saw Gregg again and heard about his family gathering in the Portslade house.

"They all came down to us," Gregg said flatly.

"How many?"

"Too many. I had to sleep on the floor. I didn't get much sleep. Noise all over the fucking house, and a lot of drinking. I had a few beers, but you should have seen how much the rest of them knocked back." Gregg shook his head in dismay, and Nick thought that he wouldn't have liked to have seen a house full of drunks. After the incident in the street with the drunk, he hated alcohol abuse. He had secretly sipped a vermouth that his aunt had brought down for Christmas and had disliked the taste.

"I drank a little as well," he said, both exaggerating and boasting.

"What?"

"Vermouth."

"Never heard of it."

When January came, Gregg proposed they should try and get in to see an X film together.

"What's on?" Nick asked.

They bought a paper and found an inviting title at the Astoria cinema: *Invasion of the Hell Creatures.*

"Let's go and see that," Nick said, and turning a few pages, they found an image of a bulbous-headed creature, carrying a female (as usual) with smoking ruins and desolation all around. The X certificate was very bold and big and the size of it alone promised a lot. Nick felt almost as excited as he had been with Gregg on the bed, but of course in a different way.

"Yes," he said.

At the Astoria, it was easier than he had expected. Gregg bought the tickets, and although there were a few people in the foyer, no one came up to question his age. He was an adult at last. Once inside the auditorium Gregg made his way to the back row of the stalls. They had to sit through a routine film first which was extremely boring and not a horror film. Then they had an ice cream each and waited for the curtains to reveal the forbidden X certificate and the warning that no one under the age of sixteen should be present.

"Here we go," Gregg said.

To their disappointment, the film was half horror and half comedy. There was also a lot of kissing with couples in cars in a wood. There were no cities crumbling with devastation. Instead they saw little creatures (was Hell that small?) scuttling across the screen. There was a confusing scene with a cow and syringe-like creature fingers poking into it, and at one point a creature eye was poked out, but the film was in black and white, so the blood was pitifully unrealistic. It was not what they had expected and Gregg turned his head to look at Nick.

"Not as good as the X I saw last May," Gregg said. "It was at the Savoy. I thought it would be difficult to get in, but I'm tall and they didn't even look at me. The cinema was packed 'cos the film was really special."

"What was it?"

"The Curse of Frankenstein."

"Was it in colour?"

"Fucking was. Real soaked-in colour, like you could feel it, and the monster! Unbelievable! His face was all criss-crossed and sewn together by Frankenstein. Saw the body parts too. Some silly woman nearly fainted in the row in front of me. She screamed and everything. She almost had to be carried out. And it was a double-X programme, not like this one. The other film was all about a prostitute in Rome. I've never seen a film about the goings on of a prostitute before. Makes me hard just thinking about it, not that you saw her cunt or anything. Pity you couldn't have seen that with me. Would've made you hard as well."

There was no one in the row of seats other than themselves, and no one to shush them for talking.

"It sounds exciting," Nick said as he imagined sitting in the cinema with them both getting an erection. His penis started to stiffen and as if reading his mind Gregg reached out, took Nick's hand and placed it on his groin. Although totally unexpected, the action was totally desired. Nick felt Gregg pushing his hand up and down against the bulge of his erection.

"Unzip me," he whispered as one of the little creatures appeared in close-up. It looked as if it was watching them and Nick realised they were about to do a punishable act in public.

"Take it out and wank me," Gregg urged. His voice was almost pleading, but as much as he wanted to, Nick couldn't do it.

"I can't," he said, and tried to draw his hand away.

"Why the fuck not?"

"The usherette may come. She has a torch."

"Don't be so fucking stupid. She's a lazy bitch. I know this cinema. I've seen her before. She never comes in during a film."

I want him, Nick thought. We are in the back row. Lovers usually use the back row to kiss. That's common knowledge, but am I a lover? I can't use that word with Gregg. It's forbidden. No one would ever let us be lovers, and certainly not in the back rows of cinemas.

Gregg was getting impatient with him now and after a minute or two of waiting for Nick to do what he had asked, he pushed Nick's hand away.

"It doesn't matter," he said. "I thought you'd want it. But what the fuck, if you're going to make it complicated. I can do it myself when this bloody awful film is over and I've gone home."

When he heard these words Nick made a decision. Gulping hard with both dread and joy at what he was about to do, he put his arm around the back of Gregg's seat and then with a sudden movement, grabbed Gregg's shoulder, forcing him to turn in astonishment towards him. Then he moved his own head close to Gregg's and in an instant was kissing him on the mouth. The action was clumsy and awkward. His own mouth was open, but Gregg's was clenched shut. There was no response from him, and Nick moved away, knowing that in that instant, he had probably destroyed everything. He stared vacantly at the screen as the creatures were encircled by a group of cars and caught in the glare of their headlamps. There was a lot of creature shrieking as the tiny little things were destroyed. Suddenly they were all gone in a puff of smoke, and the wood, not to mention the world was saved from their pathetic savagery. Gregg sat in stony silence beside him, as if he too was pinned by the car lights. The end of the film was approaching and also the end of Nick's futile attempt at being a lover. Then Gregg spoke.

"I'm not like that," he muttered. "I can't be like that."

"I'm sorry," Nick said.

The lights in the cinema would soon come on, and he did not want to face Gregg in the light. He got up from his seat and feeling frustrated and angry with himself, made his way out into the foyer. He looked at the come-on images for the film and thought how much the expectation had turned out to be a lie. Was this how it was going to be? Always, for him, if he continued to desire boys like Gregg? He knew that he was something Gregg was not, and the realisation of that difference brought tears to his eyes. He saw a possibly long life before him, and although he still believed God had nothing to do with it, he felt with a shudder that he would be consigned to Hell's eternal flames. Atheists go to hell, and so do people like me, he told himself. The ugly, protruding eyes of the creatures didn't seem to deny this as they stared apathetically in his direction. I have done the one thing, the kiss, that has made me act upon what I am. Homosexual. That is my new name now. He was not even conscious that Gregg had joined him in the foyer.

"Come on," he heard him say, "let's get out of here. You look bloody twelve years old standing there. Don't be so bloody pitiful for fuck's sake. I still like you. It's no fucking tragedy. I still want you to wank me. It doesn't mean the end for us."

He sounded awkward. His words sounded edgy and nervous and when Nick looked at him he saw that his face was pale.

"I shouldn't have acted like that," Nick said.

"Don't blame yourself. The back seat of a cinema always does it. I should have chosen the front row, but honestly I'd prefer you licking me than those creatures. Think how they look from the front row. Almost in your lap. You've got a better mug than them. Anyway, you're even better than a girlfriend. At least you pay for yourself."

"I haven't paid you for the ticket yet."

"Give me the money in the street."

Gregg's expression was blank, and he looked tired after the string of words he had just spoken: spoken with the stuttering fastness of a machine gun in a war film.

Out in the darkness of the street, they passed people waiting to go in for the evening performance. Most were couples. A few of them were openly kissing each other in the queue. The cinema will be full this evening, Nick thought.

"Do you want to go home now like you said?" Nick asked tentatively.

There was a moment's silence. They both looked at the ground. Then Gregg looked at Nick with his devastating smile and said, "Let's go on the Palace Pier. Got enough money?"

"Yes," Nick replied. "I've still got my week's pocket money."

"Then let's push pennies and see if we can get some more."

"I hope all X films are not going to be like the one we've just seen," Nick added to fuel the conversation and the returning ease between them.

"Wait 'til *The Curse of Frankenstein* comes round again. I bet the Rothbury in Portslade will get it eventually. They re-run things."

Nick thought that he wasn't really sure about Portslade, then ran on ahead, with Gregg following.

These events took place between 1957 and 1958. Now in 2015, the school that Nick went to no longer existed. The flat that he had lived in had become a school building and the tennis court was gone, replaced by a sports hall that was ugly to him. As for the Astoria, it stood, a shell of itself awaiting demolition. This too must go, he thought, and he was bitter that it must go. It had been a place of dreams and in the city, now called Brighton and Hove, there was no place any more for dreams. No more cinemas like those in the 1950s where

230

dreams came in double-bills, and where if the dreams were fulfilling enough you could sit through the programme again. A whole day could be spent in other dream-like worlds. And now this building, one of that era's last remaining monuments was to be brutally destroyed. The hell creatures were truly coming, and there would be no recall of this wonderful cinema except in books. And yet, old like him, it still stood with a solid dignity, waiting like him for its eternal oblivion to begin.

Time had etched its mark on memory.

CPSIA information can be obtained at www.ICGtesting.com
Printed in the USA
BVOW08s1048040815

411746BV00001B/29/P